THE TE

K. M. Peyton

THE TEAM

Illustrated by the author

London
OXFORD UNIVERSITY PRESS
1975

Oxford University Press, Ely House, London W.1

GLASGOW NEW YORK TORONTO MELBOURNE WELLINGTON
CAPE TOWN IBADAN NAIROBI DAR ES SALAAM LUSAKA ADDIS ABABA
DELHI BOMBAY CALCUTTA MADRAS KARACHI LAHORE DACCA
KUALA LUMPUR SINGAPORE HONG KONG TOKYO

ISBN 0 19 271372 8
© K. M. Peyton 1975
First published 1975

For Tiphanie and Philippa

Printed in Great Britain
by W & J Mackay Limited, Chatham
by Photo-litho

I

JONATHAN, watching his mother sifting through the Pony Club files, saw her suddenly not as his mother, but as a formidable, efficient, clever, middle-aged woman. It came as quite a shock. Equally suddenly, he realized that it was himself growing up that saw her like that, detaching himself from his family; it was nothing they had done. He couldn't call his mother 'Mummy' any more. It sounded too soppy. And 'Mother' was unfamiliar as yet. She wouldn't answer to 'Mum', as she was too well-bred. She herself still used the term well-bred for people, instead of just for animals; it made Jonathan curl up. In spite of this, she was all right, as mothers went.

'We're going to have a job scraping up a team for the Area Trials next summer,' she said to him.

Jonathan yawned, to hint that he wasn't terribly interested in the Pony Club any more.

'There's you and Jess, of course, in spite of your being the DC's own children, which I still find rather embarrassing. . . .'

She was the DC, which was the antediluvian term the Pony Club used for its Branch bosses. It stood for District Commissioner, and harked back to the days of the Empire. Really, Jonathan thought, it was all too childish, a big game for the ambitious adults.

'For Heaven's sake don't count me in this year,' he said peevishly. 'It messes up the whole summer.'

'Oh, don't be ridiculous,' his mother said in her cracking-down voice. 'You're not sixteen till June. You've got another whole summer to ride in the team and Railwayman's going as well as ever. I certainly won't let you drop out.'

'Thank you very much,' he said bitterly.

'Put another log on the fire. We aren't saving them any more. Jim brought another load up from Pot Wood yesterday.'

Jonathan heaved another half-hundredweight log into the ancient fire-place and watched an explosion of sparks spray across the soot-

5

dark recess. It was snowing outside, a wet slow drift spattering the dusk. He was grateful for his privilege, sitting there with his knees close to the embers, feeling the warmth striking through his thin denims. He had been selling Christmas things in the Oxfam shop all day, and now didn't even have to go out and do his own horse for the night, for there was a groom to do it for him. Having been surrounded all day by posters of starving children, his own life suddenly seemed a bit odd, even pointless. His mother, for example, frowning over her card index. As if it mattered!

'There's Peter McNair, of course, if he happens to have a decent pony when the moment comes. You can never count on his father doing the right thing. He only thinks of the money.'

'Well, it is his living,' Jonathan pointed out.

Mr. McNair was a horse-dealer, and his son's mounts came and went. The good ones mostly went, and Peter was left with the pigs.

'If only he hadn't sold that chestnut, Toadhill Flax,' Mrs. Meredith grieved. 'Peter and that animal—what a combination! They could have gone right to the very top. Made for each other. I wonder what became of that pony? I've never heard of it since it was sold.'

'No.'

'We've got the riders. What about that odd little girl—Ruth somebody, that Peter McNair's friendly with? She's keen. Doesn't know a thing, but the heart's in the right place. Her pony's a bit small though.'

'Fly-by-Night?'

'That's it. She'll want a new one this year.'

'I doubt if she'll get one. Her family's not a bit horsy. Garden full of motor bikes and she has to do a paper-round to keep herself in horse-shoes.'

'Oh.'

No privilege there. Jonathan knew that if he was Ruth Hollis, doing it all from scratch, he wouldn't ever get in any team. He was too blooming lazy. Even now, while Jim was doing Railway for the night, re-rugging him, mucking him out, filling hay-nets, he, Jonathan, sat staring into the fire . . . working in Oxfam had given him a guilt complex.

'There's some new people taken Hill Farm,' his mother was saying. 'They've got horses, and the girl's Pony Club—moved from

Suffolk, I believe. From what I've heard she might be useful. We'll have to look them up. Name of Parker.'

He grunted. As if he cared! How seriously his mother took it. Everything she did, from training her point-to-point horse to peeling potatoes, she did thoroughly, with minimum fuss and maximum efficiency. Even the Pony Club, inherited from Major Banks . . . it wouldn't be any old Pony Club now; it would be a good Pony Club, with winning teams and a serious reputation. And all for what? Jonathan groaned. His mother looked at him sharply.

'Really, Jonathan, what a mess you do look! The Sutton-Popes are coming round for drinks in an hour. Do go and put on something presentable.'

2

THE snow was coming down faster. Ruth cursed that she hadn't got Fly-by-Night in when it was still light. It was all so much easier when you could see what you were doing. She fell over his water-bucket. Blast! A cold shower of snow fell into the top of her boot and worked its way irrevocably into the lovely warm fug of her real wool red and white striped socks which Ted had given her for Christmas. She pulled the gate open, sploshing through thick mud, and Fly-by-Night was there, waiting, eager as always. Too eager.

'For Heaven's sake!'

Ruth grabbed his forelock and stopped him charging off, slipping a piece of old binder twine round his neck. He couldn't always be trusted to go straight into the stable himself, often fancying a detour round her father's vegetable patch. The stable was part of a sagging row of weatherboard sheds at the bottom of the wilderness that was euphemistically called garden; it had no electric light and all the water had to be fetched from the house, but apart from that it was all right. Better than their old house, which hadn't had a stable at all—their old house had actually been a new house, on an estate, and hadn't been given to accommodating ponies. Nor had she, Ruth thought, remembering all the crises. She hadn't known anything. It was better now, since she had got to know the McNairs. They could cope with anything, horsewise, and all her problems she took to them. Her next problem would be to find herself a new pony. This was something that she hadn't dared mention to her parents.

'I wish you would grow as fast as me,' she said to Fly, turning him into the loosebox. In the darkness he plunged his nose unerringly into the bucket of bran and pony-nuts she had prepared and she watched his dark shape, the wet black gleaming, listened to the eager, greedy scrape of his hoof on the floor. Given to worrying, she worried now about the size of her on Fly. He was only just over thirteen hands and she, having been a little thing most of her life, was suddenly, at fourteen, a little thing no longer. Not heavy, but getting tall. She knocked jumps down with her feet, after Fly had cleared them. The thought of parting with him was a dreadful black cloud in her mind. She thought about it all the time. Come the spring, and she would have to find him a new home. The thought made her feel quite ill. Peter, who had a new pony about every three months, had laughed at her fears.

'We can find you a new pony—no trouble,' he said. 'McNair guaranteed. Why do you worry so?'

'I always worry,' Ruth said.

Even to Peter she hadn't liked to mention money. McNair ponies weren't cheap, and even a friendly fifty or so knocked off for her would still be more than her father would pay.

'Hi.'

Ruth nearly jumped out of her skin. 'Talk of the devil! I was just thinking about you!'

'Lovely thoughts of course,' Peter said amiably. 'I came down to collect a magneto off Ted. I'm building a motor bike.'

'What, you too? What's wrong with horse-power?'

'Oh, makes a change from quadrupeds. More restful.'

'I haven't noticed.'

'How's your quad then?' He leaned on the stable door and frowned into the darkness. 'Too little for a big girl like you.'

'Oh, for Heaven's sake,' Ruth said, needled. 'Do you think I don't know? Don't talk about it. Talk about something else.'

'Old mother Meredith is out collecting her team *already*—wants to know what I've got that might be any good. Talk about keen! Wants to know if there's any chance of "little Ruth Hollis getting something useful this summer". That's what she said. I laughed to myself I did, thinking, "Our little Ruth's a big Ruth now and knocks all the bloody jumps down with her great big feet". Didn't say it, of course, being a tactful bloke—'

'Oh, shut up! That's what I was thinking about when you frightened the life out of me. How can I get another pony when my dad's got no money? A good pony is hundreds now—'

'Too true, my girl. Trade's very good. You'll just have to buy knacker-meat and work on it.'

'Oh, thank *you*.' They had talked about this before and Ruth knew there was no answer. Even Peter, willing as he was, couldn't *give* her one of his father's better animals.

9

'Mother Meredith doesn't realize that some people aren't natural millionaires with ten race-horses, six Range-Rovers, four gardeners, a dozen grooms, not to mention the lovely children who are perfect riders, with fantastic ponies—'

'You're getting bitter and twisted,' Peter said. 'Even exaggerating, I think. They've got one race-horse, one Range-Rover, one groom, and their ponies are really quite ordinary. Railway, for example, is just a nag. It's only Jonathan who can get him to do anything.'

'Really?'

'Yes. He won't do a thing for Jessica. She tried to do some trials with him when Jonathan was off with a broken arm or something and he wouldn't even start. Just stood up on his hind legs.'

'It's true, isn't it, that sometimes it's the two together that click —I mean, the rider and the horse, the combination—and the horse won't go for anyone else—'

'Quite right, my dear.'

'Even Fly—I don't think he's much good with another rider.'

'No, well, it helps when you're *both* mental—'

Ruth scooped some snow out of the wheelbarrow and stuffed it down the back of Peter's neck. She then flung snowballs hard into the darkness and swore a bit, and groaned, and said, 'Life's cruel and hard! I wish I was dead!'

'Tomorrow,' Peter said. 'Make me a coffee first. That's all I called for really. That and the magneto.'

They trailed up the garden through the snow, ducking under the sagging branches of the old pear trees. A new moon, thin as a wire, gave a strangely fierce light over the smoking chimney. 'I wish—I wish—' Ruth lifted her face up, not saying anything out loud, but wishing so hard that it screwed all her insides up. How could Peter possibly know that what he took quite for granted, like riding in mother Meredith's Pony Club team, would be to her like owning the sun, the moon and the stars? How he would laugh, he and that aristocratic, perfect boy, Jonathan Meredith, who had been born into it and didn't even care! How could they ever guess how *inadequate* she felt beside them?

'Did Mrs. Meredith really mention me, like you said?' The uplifting iota of optimism in the conversation with Peter returned, halfway up the garden path. She stopped and stared at him very earnestly in the moonlight. She said, 'I mean—as if I might—'

'She thinks your heart's in the right place. I said, "Yes, halfway down her chest on the left," and she said—'

'Oh, I hate you! You're a swine—'

'And she said, "if *little* Ruth could get a proper animal" and did I know that the Archers were selling Nightlight—'

'For nine hundred pounds,' Ruth put in.

'Yes, with his shoes on, mind you, and a full set of teeth—'

'Groan, groan,' Ruth said.

'Oh, well. That's all she said really. And had we met some people called Parker come to live at Hill Farm.'

'And had we?'

'No, we hadn't. But we'd heard say of them that they be very peculiar, consisting of one mother, one daughter and thousands of animals all moved in with the furniture—horses, beds, geese, wardrobes, hens, ironing-boards, goats, armchairs all in together.'

'You're making this up?'

'No, I be not.'

They went into the kitchen, where Ted had his usual bits of motor bike all over the table and the transistor going full blast.

'Get to the stove, woman,' Peter said to Ruth, 'and make warm nourishing drinks for your menfolk. I have to go out into the snow by bicycle shortly, struggle home through the blizzard and tuck forty horses up for the night.'

'Why? What's your dad doing?'

'Gone to Newmarket. George's night off, Maggie's got flu, Mother won't. That leaves—guess who?'

'Good for you. These Parker people, what's the girl like? I mean, how old?'

'Thin and tough,' Ted said. 'Like chewed leather. Not my type at all.'

'Why, when did you see her?'

'Yesterday. My motor bike and her horse took instant aversion and she was very impolite. I wouldn't have anything to do with her, Ruth. She's not a lady. Not our class of person at all.'

'Oh—you—' Ruth gave up. It wasn't any use trying to make sense out of the boys when they got into their moods. Peter had lived with them for a time once and was as good as a brother. He and Ted got on, although Ted was twenty to Peter's fifteen. She would have to ride past Hill Farm until she met up with this Parker girl, and find out what she was like. It would be nice to have someone to ride with—as long as she proved better than ghastly Pearl in the village, who had dropped ponies now for boys, and sold her lovely animals—Milky Way as a brood mare and Woodlark to someone who could manage her.

'This horse she was riding,' Peter said to Ted, serious again, 'what was it like?'

'They all look the same to me. Four legs, a head and things.'

'Chestnut?'

'Bright brown. Not ginger, I wouldn't say.'

'Flashy? White stockings?'

'Its legs were in a ditch, hence the rude words.'

'Someone said her horse is called Bright Morning, and if it's the same Bright Morning we had once it's a snorter.'

'Snorter?' Ruth queried.

'Very good nag. Woman that bought it—now I come to think of it, she was called Parker, or Perkins or some such similar—she had an eye for a horse. I remember my dad saying. She was a right weirdie, but she knew a good one when it wasn't obvious. Bright Morning was one of those. Dad said he'd give her a job if she wanted one.'

Ruth felt depressed, seeing her tiny chance of getting in a team one unimaginable day retreat perceptibly farther away.

'Perhaps it's gone to the bad in spite of her good eye,' she said hopefully. 'If it was in a ditch—'

'Any quite normal person,' Peter said, 'would get in a ditch if they saw Ted coming towards them on a motor bike.'

3

THEODORA Parker, who was always called Thea, had discovered that the roofs of the Hill Farm stables let in water like a sieve. The snow floated down from the rafters and hissed on the hot glass of the hurricane lamp. Bright Morning looked cold and cross.

'Some Bright Morning! More like Wet December Night, you poor old brute.'

She sighed. The whole place was falling down, the house as well, which is why they had been able to afford it. The house was sliding down the hill, the milkman had said, cheerfully. Had been for years. Perhaps when it reached the stable, Thea thought, it would stop. Her mother didn't bother about things like that. 'I think it's all charming,' she said looking at the mossy tiles and the quaint (leaking) gables and the lopsided (leaking) windows and plunging off in her wellington boots through the mud to survey the five acres that went with it. The stables and barns were very picturesque, full-stop, Thea thought. The yards were liquid mud and waist-high rosebay willow-herb inadequately hiding the rusty remains of a tractor and an old hay-cart.

'We can paint that up and sell it to an antique shop,' Mrs. Parker said.

'What, the tractor?' Thea wasn't as optimistic. She knew that her mother's eyes did not see what she did not want to know about, and the mess would remain unless she, Thea, cleared it up. Now, in the December snow, she didn't think she had the strength. Even to move Bright Morning . . . the driest part of the barn was beyond where the removals men had dumped the big galvanized feed bins, and to get Bright Morning through . . . he might be on the thin side, but he wasn't that thin. The goats didn't matter so much, and Minnie, the cow, was in another shed which had no floor but a reasonable roof. Dido, the little pony, was out in the yard. She didn't like being shut in, but had plenty of shelter there if she wanted it, and a large hay-net to tug at.

'It's only you, you poor suffering nag.'

It took her two hours to clear out a new loosebox, move the bins, which nearly killed her, and put up some rails to keep the horse in. Even the straw in the stack was wet and mouldy and had to be sorted. The lamplight was hopeless. She felt like crying, but was too practical to indulge. It hadn't ever been like this when her father and Mick were still alive, but it was obviously going to be like this quite a lot in this new place. Bright Morning, placid as old Minnie in the stable (but not out) snuffled round his new quarters, and took a snatch of hay. Thea moved the water-bucket, tied her rickety rails up with binder twine, and fell over one of the goats as it moved up to investigate the new arrangements. The lamp was almost out, the glass all smoked up. She retrieved it, and retreated out into the snow. She felt limp with weariness. Her mother had milked Minnie, thank God. She got the cow some water, and a bucket for Dido, and struggled back through the yard towards the house. The snow was coming down fast, and there were stars showing at the same time and a thin moonlight giving a stagey effect. Seen under the veil of snow, the old house looked magical, but when she got indoors there were buckets on the floor to catch the drips. Her mother was arranging some wan sticks in a white jug on the kitchen mantelpiece.

'Oh, look, Thea, I've found some winter jasmine! It'll come out in the warm, I'm sure. Isn't it lovely?'

'What's for supper?'

'Oh, heavens, I'd forgotten—it's quite late, isn't it? I think there are two of Rosie's eggs on that basket-chair—didn't I put them there? Yes, here they are. They're not laying very well—the move's upset them, I suppose. Shall we boil them? The cooker's a bit peculiar, only one ring seems to work. I don't know why. I haven't found the toaster since we moved.'

She floated in her characteristic way round the kitchen, a thin, dreaming, drifting woman whom Thea sometimes found difficult to love. Now was one of those times. When her father had been alive, her mother's vagueness had been endearing and amusing; her father's essential strength and practicality and intelligence had needed no support. Now Thea was finding that she had to take her father's place when it came to the things that mattered and although she recognized that she was by nature tough like her father, it didn't mean that she was noble enough not to resent the burden.

Faced with a house that was falling down, leaking stables, sagging gates, broken fences and all that mud, she would have preferred to take her mother's refuge in flower-arranging. Now she had to find the toaster out of one of the unopened crates that were stacked under the window, and see about getting someone to fix the cooker, and find a better way of getting Bright Morning in and out of his loosebox . . .

She fetched the nice warm eggs, Rosie's valiant effort in her new surroundings, and reached for a saucepan. Her mother's straggling vase gleamed here and there with yellow stars of jasmine against the old white plaster and, seeing them, she unaccountably felt better.

'It'll be lovely in the summer.'

Optimism, after all, was not her mother's prerogative.

4

'I T's not horse-meat we're after,' Ted said. 'It's machinery.'

'There's no harm in looking,' Ruth said.

'No—well—' Ted was dubious, with quite good reason. He had come to the market for an auction of second-hand motor bikes, and Ruth, knowing that it was horses' day as well, had come with him 'to have a look'. 'For fun,' she said. 'Huh,' Ted grunted. 'Some fun.' Every time the knacker made a bid she burst into tears. And if they were thin and pathetic, she cried. Even the hens.

'Look, I'll see you here then, about an hour. My lot should come up about eleven.'

'I'll just wander about,' Ruth said. 'All right.'

They parted, and Ruth made a bee-line for the cattle-market. It was an awful day, the half-hearted snow making thick sludge underfoot. Ruth didn't like the market much, and its effect on her, but she wanted to see what you could get for the money. She was a bit out of touch with prices. And the market, with all its attendant risks, might be her only chance of picking up a larger pony for what she would get when she sold Fly-by-Night. Chance was the operative word. She wasn't rich enough to buy a McNair guaranteed. She would just have to put her faith in God and take a gamble. She thought she would come for a few weeks and get the hang of prices and what was available, and then, when it was spring and she had sold Fly-by-Night, she would get Peter to come and help her pick another. By then she would be able to guess roughly what she could get for her money and, with Peter and a lot of luck, she might not make too bad a mistake. After all, she had bought Fly-by-Night without knowing anything at all, for almost nothing, and he had turned out all right.

She bought a catalogue and made for the stalls where the horses were tied. Some were still arriving, the horse-boxes champing and sneezing backwards up the yard to unload, the usual motley collection of farmish-looking people wandering about, hunched into sheepskin jackets or khaki parkas, with pinched damp noses and cold hands fumbling to read the lot numbers. It wasn't really horse-selling time—the hunters had gone earlier and the ponies and hacks would go in the spring: these were dregs, the ones who couldn't afford to be kept any more, or were too impossible to put up with any longer. Ruth recognized immediately a famous bolter, and an ex-point-to-point horse whose legs had gone. She felt miserable instantly, aware that nobody in their right mind could possibly buy such horses—some rich old lady, perhaps, with lots of grass going spare? She glanced round hopefully, but there seemed to be a dearth of such applicants. The faces she saw were cold and hard and suspicious, like her own. If she was rich, she would buy them all, she knew she would . . . they weren't like motor bikes, in a heap . . . oh, God, she wished she hadn't come! She'd never do it week after week, and the knackerman's lorry parked there. It was awful. In a minute she was going to cry.

She made her way round a double trailer unloading a pair of Shetland ponies and went slowly down the row of shaggy rumps, rejecting mentally, not attracted, and feeling relieved because of it and disappointed both together. A chestnut backside glowed out of the murk and a woman standing beside it said, 'I've had it run out and it's lame as a duck.'

'Oh, mother, we don't want it anyway. Nothing else until the spring. We can't cope.' The girl she spoke to answered Ted's description of 'thin and leathery' for the Parker girl. Ruth, having seen her once in the distance, thought it was her, but wasn't sure. She stood eavesdropping.

'The groom said it had navicular, but it hasn't. None of the symptoms. It's had a knock, a sore shoulder or something. It's bound to go cheap, lame and in that condition. But it's only eight and a lovely type. Real Welsh cob, but not too heavy.'

'Yes,' said the girl. 'But it's no good getting carried away. We've got to get the place tidied up before we import any more animals. There's not another dry loose box, for a start.'

She sounded impatient. Her mother patted the cob and said, 'It's a good sort. You couldn't go wrong. Anyone with eyes to see —and he'll go for a song, because—'

'Yes, mother, but we haven't got a song and we don't want a gelding. A mare perhaps.'

'No. Oh well. Let's go and look at the poultry. We really

17

ought to have a new cockerel for the spring. We're getting too inbred.'

Ruth watched them wander away. Everything they had said, and the way they looked, fitted in with their being the Parkers of Hill Farm. Mrs. Parker who had a fantastic eye for a horse. . . .

Ruth's eyes switched to the chestnut. She felt that she was on very dangerous ground, and not wholly in control of herself. Suppose—

Suppose nothing. She thought she ought to walk away now, but she went up to the pony's head and gazed at it long and hard. Something stirred, way back in the recesses of her mind. The pony turned and looked back at her, and although it had a sad, resigned, beaten demeanour, she saw it, strangely, full of spirit and strength, as once—

'You—' She stared hard at the pony. She felt herself getting out of hand again, the excitement stirring.

'I know you,' she said to him. 'You are—' Or was she dreaming? Was it just wishful thinking? As if she had a dream pony in her mind and was forcing it to materialize, just because—once—there had been a real chestnut pony like this one, belonging to Peter McNair, who had gone round the Hunter Trial course like a Grand National winner and won all the rosettes going? She tried to forget the conversation she had overheard and looked at the pony coolly and critically. It was about fourteen and a half hands high, and a bright copper chestnut with a flaxenwhite mane and tail, both very long and bedraggled. It was, beneath its sad condition, a very powerfully-built pony, deep through and wide across the chest, short-backed and compact; in fact, so rough and in its thick winter coat, it looked a miniature cart-horse. But Ruth had learned to look beneath winter coats, and she saw in this pony everything she wanted to see: speed and courage and stamina and —'Stop it'. She shut her eyes. She was getting carried away, and it was hopeless. She opened her eyes again. The more she looked, the more she was sure that this was Peter McNair's old pony, Toadhill Flax. There was no name in the catalogue, only a number. How to find out?

'Do you know this pony's name?' She asked a man in a brown overall who seemed to be organizing where to put horses.

'Goldie,' he said. 'Come from a man called Richards.'

'Do you know anything else about him?'

'Not much. The girl was never interested. Scared, I think she was. He trots out lame, that's all I know.'

'Why's he lame?'

'Not my department, that.'

Ruth examined the pony's legs and feet, but could find no clues. The pony was unshod, but its hooves were sound enough. Packed with mud, there was not much to be seen in his feet. No lumps inside the pasterns, or down his legs. If only she knew more! But lameness—it was like a human backache, caused by any of a hundred reasons. It could be nothing, or fatal. She grovelled about feverishly, and the pony put down its head and lipped at her hair, tickling the back of her neck. It was gentle, sad, thin. Oh, God, she wanted it! She was seized with a quite uncontrollable fit of the shivers. She *must*! There would never be a chance like this again. Not to get a pony like Toadhill Flax for a song. It was him, she was sure.

'Toad! Are you Toad?' That's what Peter had called him. Said he jumped like a toad. The pony blew on her cold hands and took the bone button of her duffel coat in its teeth.

'You are. I'm sure you are.'

She looked at all the other animals, but they were just nothing. Too big, too small, too rough, too weedy, just nothing. But every time she came back to the chestnut again he was more and more desirable. The shivers wouldn't go away. She knew Ted had a hundred pounds in his pocket, to buy a junk motor bike. He had sold his old one. He was quite well off; he had told her so. She kept thinking of this. Eleven o'clock. She walked up and down through the slush. The first ponies were going off to be sold, but there was plenty of time. Too much. She wished it was quite impossible, then it would have been easier. But the thought of Ted's money needled her.

'If he's bought a new bike, it's finished. It's impossible. But if he hasn't—if he's still got the money—' She couldn't stop thinking about Ted's money, shaking and trembling. She felt sick.

At eleven o'clock she went back to their rendezvous, and he came five minutes later. He looked gloomy.

'Load of rubbish.'

'You haven't bought one?'

'No. Waste of time. Only one I wanted went for double what I've got.'

'You've still got it then?'

'What?'

'The money.'

'Oh. Yes. You done then?'

'No. There's a pony—Ted, *please*—' She was hopping up and down from one foot to the other, white as a sheet. 'Please, Ted, come and look. It's the chance of a lifetime. It will never, never, never happen again.'

'Oh, my Gawd, Ruth! You can't.'

Ruth started to cry.

'More than my life's worth.'

'Just come and look.'

She started to drag him across the market. 'Look,' he said. 'I'm going to get married. I need the money. I can't—'

'It's only until I sell Fly-by-Night. Just for a fortnight—just a loan. There's no harm in it at all, don't you see? You know I've grown out of Fly. If I get another pony for the same money as he's worth, what's the problem? I'll give it back to you the minute he's sold. Next week. Mr. McNair would give me the money for him— you know he would—you can't say no—'

Ted stamped after her, scowling horribly. Ruth, having decided that Fate was on her side, was carried along by a quite irresistible passion, which Ted, knowing his sister, recognized. He knew she could go potty at times, and this was one of them.

'What on earth will Mother and Dad say? They'll go raving, if you arrive home with an animal. I'll get the blame—they'd never have let you come without—'

'It's no different from a motor bike! Can't you see, if I miss this chance—this is *saving* money—'

Ted couldn't see it, but suffered himself to be dragged over to examine the chestnut pony. He realized that he wasn't going to persuade Ruth out of her fixation; the onus was on him. He wasn't very happy about it.

'It'll probably go for more than I've got,' he said hopefully.

'No, it won't. It's lame.'

'Lame? Well, heavens, you don't want a lame pony!'

'Yes, this one I do. I do *want* him! Can't you see, Ted, it will never happen again—this is one of McNair's—it was Peter's old pony, and it was fantastic when he had him! But now it's fallen on hard days and it'll go cheap.'

'If it's lame they ought to give it away. What about vet's bills ?'

'Oh, don't! Peter will know what's wrong. It's only a knock or something. You will, Ted, won't you ?'

'I don't want to hang about. I've got to be back at the garage at one.'

'Oh, he'll go before then. Look, he's number twenty-four. They're up to fifteen already. Please, Ted, just let's go and see what happens. It can't do any harm—'

'Oh, can't it ?' Ted said darkly. The girl was a maniac. They all looked the same to him, except that the chestnut pony, when it was led into the ring, was indubitably lame. There weren't many buyers, and one or two of the ruder ones jeered when the pony's description was read out. Ted looked at Ruth. She was shaking like a leaf. He felt doomed.

'Ted,' she whispered. Her fingers closed round his wrist. '*Please!*' Her hand was icy. Great shining tears brimmed in her maniacal eyes. She was a raving loony. The bidding went up to sixty-five and he bid seventy. It was like bidding for his own bit of rope at the execution. Her grip was cutting off his circulation. He removed his hand, and a man with a pipe bid seventy-five. The auctioneer looked at Ted and he nodded and the auctioneer said, 'Eighty over here.' The chestnut stood in the middle of the ring, drooping and dejected, and the man on its halter gave him a chuck and walked him round again. Another man came in at eighty-five and the bidding went up to ninety-five, which was to Ted. The man with the pipe bid a hundred.

The auctioneer looked at Ted.

Ted looked at Ruth.

'A hundred and ten!' she shouted out.

Ted opened his mouth and she kicked him, agonizingly, on the knee. Nobody else said anything. Ted hopped about, muttering, and the auctioneer said, 'A hundred and ten to the gentleman in the leather coat.'

'To this lunatic,' Ted said. 'To this flaming little nut-case. You are now bidding with money we don't possess.'

'No advance on one hundred and ten ?'

Long silence. Ted had his hand on Ruth's neck, ready to gag her.

'Sold to the gentleman over here.' The auctioneer nodded at Ted. Ruth swayed and let out all her breath and looked to Ted as if she was physically shrinking before his gloomy eyes. He gave her an angry shake.

'You've got ten quid stashed away, I take it?'

'No,' she said.

'Where are we going to find it then?'

'I don't know,' she whispered.

They went up to the clerk and Ted said, 'Keep this child as hostage while I go and find the money. If I don't come back, sell it.'

'Sir?' The clerk looked puzzled. Ted went away and left Ruth standing waiting. The pony had been tied up again. Now it had happened she felt numb and terrified. She was so frightened at what she had done that she was rooted to the spot. She felt that nothing was real. She was so cold she couldn't feel her extremities at all. Her heart was thudding away heavily, pushing her petrified blood around her pipes, while her brain registered nil, axed solid. It was in the right place, she remembered, her heart—

'We've got to be all cleared up by one,' the clerk said. 'What's your lot number?'

'Twenty-four.'

Ted was ages. Everything was sold by the time he came back. He paid the clerk one hundred and ten pounds in cash, and Ruth took the receipt.

'Where did you get it?' she whispered.

'I went down to the garage and got an advance on my wages,' he said. 'And look—remember, it's all your pigeon. I—'

'Yes, truly, I promise. I'll take all the blame, and I promise you'll have the money in no time.'

'I must be raving. How are you going to get home?'

'I'll have to walk.'

'You'll be all day! Can't think of anything else though. You are a nutter, Ruth! I wonder what Dad'll say? And Mum? It's me that's going to get the rocket. They know you don't know any better, but I'm supposed to be of responsible years. They'd never have let you out alone, and now—' He rolled his eyes. 'Stone the crows! I'll stay away till it's all blown over.'

'I won't be home for hours,' Ruth said in a small voice.

'No, well I won't be home for even longer. You all right?' He peered at her anxiously. 'Hadn't you better have something to eat before you set off? Cheese roll or something?'

He went over to the van and bought her a cheese roll and a cup of tea, then he went back to work and Ruth was left with her pony. Almost everyone else had gone, mostly in horse-boxes, and the skinny chestnut looked forlorn, tied up alone. His pale, feathery legs were caked with slush and mud. Ruth went up to him and gave him half her cheese roll which he ate eagerly, then she untied him and set off for home. It was snowing softly, but without any wind. The pony walked at her side in its resigned, gentle way, its lameness not too evident at the walk, not bad enough to worry about too much, but not good enough to risk riding. He didn't mind the traffic, even buses. Ruth kept her head down and tried to stop her thoughts from wandering. Every time she stopped concentrating, they reared up with such awful visions that she felt quite faint with horror. The main fear was that this pony wasn't Toadhill Flax at all, but some hopeless dud with an uncurable foot ailment, only fit for the knacker's. She kept telling herself that Mrs. Parker, with her eye for a horse, thought him desirable, and that the man with the pipe, who looked very intelligent, had thought him worth a hundred pounds at least. But if he wasn't Toad. . . .

She realized that she had taken a colossal gamble. Carried away, back there, she had known it was a gamble, but now, with eight cold miles to think about it, she could feel her fear hardening, the blood growing sluggish, the nerves growing cold.

'Toad!' she said to him. He took no notice. She tried 'Goldie' in the same tone of voice, but he took no notice of that either. He plodded obediently at her side, with no sign at all of the dance and spirit that had so distinguished him in his early days. When Peter had had him—if it was him—he had been all fire, shining and pulling and dancing about, mad to go. With nothing else to think about, and all the time in the world for the brain to run riot, she felt her horrors growing.

'PETER! Is that you? I got a wrong number before—'

'Hi.'

'It's Ruth here. I want you to help me. In fact, I'm a bit desperate. Please, please—'

'What on earth are you on about?'

'I've bought a pony and I want you to come and look at it.'

'What, now?'

'Yes.'

'It's pitch dark and snowing. Have you noticed?'

'Yes. Well, I'm standing under a lamp-post—I'm in the phone-box at Ash Corner. You've only got to get on your bike—five minutes.'

'You mean you've got the pony with you?'

'Yes.'

'In the phone-box?'

'Well, just his front bit. I'm on my way home, and I thought— as I'm so near your house, you could come—'

'Can't you bring him up here?'

'I'm dropping. I've walked all the way from Marshfield. To come up to you will put an extra two miles on—'

'You're raving, girl. Walked all the way from Marshfield? In this awful weather! You bought it in the market, you mean?'

'Yes. Impulse buy.'

'Crikey! You *are* raving. Why do you want me to see it then? It's not much good now, is it, if you've already bought it? What am I supposed to do? Assure you it's lovely?'

'I think it's Toadhill Flax. I want you to tell me.'

'Toad.' Long pause. Peter's voice changed abruptly. 'I'll come down. You'll stay there till I come?'

'Yes. Fast as possible. I'm freezing.'

It took him ten minutes. The pony was grazing on the roadside verge and Ruth was standing by his head, teeth chattering. It was four o'clock and dark already, the snow still falling with its soft, wet insistence. Peter trained his bike dynamo on the pony's head, and bent over, reaching for the halter.

'Toad, Toad! Come up, fellow. Let's have a look at you! Oh, you old devil, you! My beauty—'

'Is it?'

'Oh, yes, of course it is! My old beauty! You couldn't mistake him in a hundred years! How could you be so stupid—'

'I *did* think it was! But then I was scared.' Ruth felt like bursting into tears of relief. She was so tired and frozen and hungry and scared; Peter's assurance made her feel better instantly. She beamed at him in the lamplight, almost laughing.

'A hundred and ten pounds! I thought it was, and Ted had the money for a motor bike—I made him buy him! Oh, Peter! It's wonderful! I can't believe it!'

She expected Peter to respond, applauding her good fortune, but he was strangely subdued.

'What are you going to do with him? Why don't you bring him up to our place for the night?'

'But from here, it's no farther to go home. I only rang you because I was desperate to know, and it was easier for you to come just this far, instead of to my house. Besides, my parents don't know yet. There's going to be a God Almighty row when I get home.'

'Bring him up to ours then, and tell them in the morning. You must be knackered.'

'No. I'd rather get it over tonight.'

Peter shrugged. He put his hand out and caressed a lock of the bedraggled mane. 'He looks awful. Whatever have they been doing to him?' His voice was soft and miserable. 'He never deserved that.'

'He's lame too.'

'Poor old devil!'

'But he'll be wonderful—when he's fed and fit again! He'll be like he used to be. I can't believe it.'

Peter muttered something, and stood there, just looking. Ruth, wanting to rejoice after her awful hours of doubt, was dampened again by his attitude, and rather surprised.

'Aren't you pleased to see him again?'

He shrugged again. 'Bring him up to our place. Just for tonight.'

25

'But it's no good putting it off—for me, I mean. I want to get tonight over.'

'You could tell them tonight, and still have him at our place. Dad will run you home in the car.'

Ruth looked at Peter in the lamplight. He looked very odd, she realized, almost shocked. She knew he was a moody character, and that his good humour and banter could subside into long periods of gloom and resentment, but she hadn't expected this reaction from him in this particular circumstance. She had been expecting him to join in a general rejoicing. His insistence that she take the pony to his home seemed to her rather like a taking-over attitude.

'No,' she said. 'I want him in my stable.' The vision of the ill-used pony going into her own loose box out of the snow, with the lamp casting its warm welcome and the straw heaped up, clean and ready, the hay-net already filled, had sustained her with a lovely anticipation during the whole of the long walk home. It was her dream come true—even truer now that she knew the pony really was Toad. To have that moment denied her, even with the great

axe to fall as soon as she went up the garden and into the kitchen and told her mother what she had done, was not to be considered. The McNair loose boxes might be far more splendid, but they were not where Toad belonged any longer.

She pulled the pony's head up out of the grass and turned him back on to the road.

'Thank you for coming.' She felt awkward. 'I'm terribly relieved it is him.'

Peter gave a cross sigh and got on his bike again.

'It's okay,' he said, and cycled away quickly, head-down, into the darkness. Ruth watched the red light receding down the lane, and stepped out again, before she got frozen solid. It was dangerous now, in the dark without a light, and she hurried the pony on, keeping on the verge wherever there was one. Fortunately it wasn't a busy road, and Toad's white tail was a help in the headlights. She felt very tired, her thoughts no longer very coherent. Down the long hill, over the main road, through the village and down the muddy lane to the lights of her own house shining through the trees: it was only overwhelming relief she felt now, creeping down the garden on the grass so that her mother in the kitchen wouldn't come out at the sound of hooves, pushing open the stable-door. Fly, waiting at the gate, flung out a piercing

whinny at the presence of the stranger. Ruth felt a guilty pang for him, pushed out of his place. She shut the door on Toad, and went to get the feeds. A bucket of nuts would soon shut Fly up, and he wouldn't care if he was in or out as long as he got fed. There was a shed in the field he could shelter in. Toad could have his hay on the floor; she could tie the hay-net in the shed for Fly. Although it was snowing, there was no wind, and no harm for Fly to stay out. She stumbled about, unable to light the lamp because the matches were in the house. The stable unaccountably seemed to have shrunk now that Toad occupied it instead of Fly, but by the time she had laid the straw out and got the hay, Toad looked comfortable enough. Unlike most horses in a strange place, he settled down immediately, eating fast. Ruth stood by the door for a minute, listening to the lovely chomping noise of a horse in the darkness of the stable, warm and sheltered for the night, an accomplishment that never ceased to give her a feeling of great satisfaction and security and peace, then turned towards the house. She could not enjoy Toad to the full until the ordeal of telling her parents was over. It was no good putting it off.

28

'You *are* late! I was beginning to think something had happened to you,' her mother said, as she stood on the door-mat, blinking. 'Whatever have you been doing? You're soaked through! Oh, you idiot child, you look like a drowned rat! You haven't been out in this all day!'

'Yes.'

'I thought you'd be at Peter's or somewhere. Whatever have you been doing? Get those things off!'

'I've bought a pony.'

'What with, may I ask? Your pocket-money? Give me your boots. And your socks.'

'We bought it with Ted's motor bike money,' Ruth persisted doggedly, wanting to get it over. 'It's in the stable.'

Her mother looked at her acidly. 'This is a joke? You aren't serious?'

'I am serious. You can go and have a look.'

Her mother straightened up and stared at her.

'I shall sell Fly straight away,' Ruth got in quickly, desperately. 'I shall get the money back as soon as he's sold and it will all be the same, just the same. Only the pony's a bit bigger. It's Peter's old pony, you remember—that chestnut called Toad. It's a bargain —I just had to—'

'Ruth!'

Ruth froze. She hadn't expected it to be any different, only it was hard to take. Her mother wasn't one of those noble, understanding, sympathetic mothers that one came across in books: she thought horses a great waste of money anyway, even Fly-sized ones, and the time Ruth spent on them wasted, when she could have been doing something 'useful' (unstipulated). Ruth sat down and tried not to listen, but it was very pointed and bitter, and quite a lot of it was true. She started to cry, overcome with weariness and emotion, and at the height of it, her sobs increasing and her mother's invective scaling fresh pinnacles of invention (or was it truth?) the door opened again and Ted came in.

'Evening all.'

His mother rounded on him instantly. 'You're to blame, of course! We all know Ruth has absolutely no sense of responsibility at all, but *you*—you're old enough to know better! You—'

'Look, it was my money, not yours.' Ted's voice was very firm. 'You're losing nothing. We all know she's a lunatic, but sometimes

29

she has to be humoured. She'll sell Fly, and everything will be the same as before.'

'Yes, and don't tell me a larger pony isn't going to eat more, cost more, need a new saddle, this, that and the other—we all know it's true. We've had it over and over again—'

Ted's arrival just set her off again. Ted took off his crash-helmet and started to unwind all the multitude of clothes that enveloped him, and his mother out of habit started to collect them up and shake them out and hang them up to dry and after a bit she began to run out of things to say. Ted staunchly defended Ruth, and Ruth began to realize that the awful deed was getting accepted. Ted was marvellous, like a great brick wall to lean on. She stopped crying.

'Go and get in the bath. You'll catch your death,' her mother threw at her, and she escaped gratefully, crawling up the stairs like a fox which has escaped the hounds. When she came out of the bathroom Ted, waiting to go in, said to her, 'I still want my money back all the same. For all I'm so gracious, don't think—'

'No, of course not. I'll sell Fly at once.'

'It's safe downstairs now. Your dinner's ready. Battle smoke clearing, only distant rumble of retreating guns.'

It was a strange, uneasy evening. Ruth, tired to death, could not stop her brain revolving at great speed, sending out all manner of excitements, scares, and aspirations. Persecuted, both by her own thoughts and her mother's, she grabbed a coat and fled back down the garden and hung over the stable-door, taking in soothing breaths of hay and warm horse.

'Toad!' she whispered. 'Toad, come here.'

She saw the pony's white blaze turn in the darkness, his head come up from the pile of hay on the floor. The steady munching paused. 'Toad! Please.'

He turned round and came to the door, pushing his muzzle at her outstretched hand. She stroked his warmth, ran her hand down his neck beneath the white, tangled mane. Everything was all right in that instant, the jangling fears laid to rest. He was gentle and kind. She remembered his courage, the way he had galloped and jumped for Peter. She had never seen him refuse, ever, all the time Peter had had him. It was all worth it; she knew she had been right.

Out in the darkness, Fly whinnied. A slightly indignant, sad whinny. Ruth felt guilty. Nothing was ever easy, it seemed; she could not gain a single step without pain to match. Selling Fly—the glib words had passed her lips several times that day, but the fact of actually doing it had not really sunk in at all. She had not pictured parting with him, seeing his jaunty tail disappear down the drive for the last time. Stroking Toad, she felt troubled about the prospect. She couldn't think of anyone, off-hand, good enough to deserve Fly. Even if Mr. McNair took him, it would only be for resale. And he, being a dealer, did not consider very much what sort of a person he sold his ponies to, as long as they paid. Look what had happened to Toad.

Ruth took her leave of Toad. As she went up the garden, pressing footsteps into the new snow, she heard Fly whinny again, plaintively. And Toad answered him. 'It's nothing,' she said to herself. 'Proper horsy people buy and sell all the time. It's just that I'm so sentimental and mushy, the way I carry on.' It was just something she would have to face. She was too excited to sleep, and it seemed to her that Fly whinnied all night, standing forsaken in the snow.

The next morning Ruth went down to the stable to gaze in rapture at her new pony, feed him and muck him out, and give Fly another hay-net. She still felt as if yesterday was a dream: it had all happened so quickly that it was difficult to adjust. She felt stiff and tired, and not quite all present. When she got back to the house, she was surprised to find Peter and his father in the kitchen, drinking coffee with her mother.

'Hullo, Ruth,' said Mr. McNair. 'We were driving over to Northend, and Peter insisted we drop in—see this nag of yours. Old Toad, eh? That's a coincidence, if you like.'

Ruth beamed at him. 'Yes, isn't it wonderful? I'd love you to look at him. He's lame and I don't know what it is. Not much, I don't think.' She had convinced herself of this.

'Yes, we can have a look. No trouble. They don't come as good as him very often.'

'He wasn't easy,' Peter said.

Ruth looked at Peter anxiously. He looked gloomy, staring into his coffee-cup.

'He was young then, surely? He seems very quiet now.'

'He was always quiet in the stable,' Peter said. 'Riding him is another matter.'

31

Ruth frowned. 'I've improved quite a lot,' she said. And even as she said it, she knew that she would never be able to ride like Peter, however hard she worked at it. Peter rode better than anyone she had ever come across. And if he said Toad was difficult—this was something she hadn't thought about, strangely enough. She had supposed, because the pony looked so poor and thin and subdued, that he would be quite easy to ride. She remembered now that this was by no means always the case.

'Are you trying to put me off?'

'Yes,' Peter said.

Ruth couldn't fathom his attitude and chose to ignore it. She had enough to worry about for the present.

'Buying a pony like that!' her mother said. 'Just as if it was a bar of chocolate. A hundred pounds, on the spur of the moment! Not many people have the opportunity.'

'I would give you a hundred pounds for that pony here and now, Mrs. Hollis,' McNair said. 'I don't think you need think she's thrown the money away. Whether it will prove to be the pony for *her* is another matter.'

'I still consider it a very irresponsible way to behave. Another cup of coffee?'

'I'll have one,' said Ruth. She didn't like the way the conversation was going. 'Peter?'

'No.'

'No, thank you,' Ruth corrected him. He glowered at her. 'What are you going to Northend for? Horses?'

'We're going to see some jumping ponies a woman's got. Says she can't afford to keep 'em anymore,' Mr. McNair said.

In spite of the fact that Peter had once run away from home because his father made him ride too much, (before and after school while there was any daylight left) he still—having made the peace —spent a good deal of time in his father's trade. McNair had a very good reputation and anyone who had enough money went to him for children's ponies, especially anything with a bit of form for the show-jumping ring. Most of these ponies were bought green and got going by Peter, or else they were bought very cheap because through ignorant forcing they had become unmanageable, and Peter had the job of re-schooling them. McNair had employed any amount of girls to help with the riding, but none of them were as good as Peter. Some of the ponies sold on reverted to their former bad habits after a short while with an indifferent rider, but McNair would take them back and supply another, never losing either his good reputation or his profit.

They drank the coffee, and went down the garden to the stable. Toad put his head out and whinnied.

'He knows me,' Peter said.

'Rubbish,' Ruth said. 'That was for me.'

'Let's have a look at him then,' Mr. McNair shot back the bolt on the door. 'Get a halter, Ruth. Let's see this lameness. Trot him out.'

McNair's professionalism was a great comfort to Ruth. The way he looked at the animal, felt him, examined his mouth and his legs and his feet: it was like Ted and his motor bikes. She admired specialist knowledge. It impressed her enormously, and made her wish that she was good at something other than mushy poetry and history, neither of which impressed anybody.

'Wants worming,' McNair said. 'We've got some stuff in the car—I'll give you a couple of boxes before we go. Then some good feeding—he'll be a new animal by spring. The lameness—that's in this near fore. You can't see anything but I think there's some infection, a prick, and its infected inside. Get Eddie to come over and have a look. He'll probably cut it and you'll find pus inside. It's nothing much, I'm pretty sure.'

Much cheered, Ruth saw them off at the gate. Peter sat slumped in the front seat of the smart Mercedes, professional-looking in jodhpurs, very distant. Ruth was puzzled by his attitude, but forgot it during the day, busy with telephoning Eddie, the farrier, and attending to the operation when he came down after lunch. Mr. McNair's diagnosis was proved correct. Eddie found the infection and opened it up and cleaned it. They packed the hoof with a hot bran poultice, and Ruth learned how to secure it.

'Be right as rain in a day or two. Then you bring him up and we'll get him shod. He's a good one, this. I remember him well.'

Ruth, warmed by the compliment, chilled by the bill, which she paid out of her Christmas present hoard, spent the last hour of daylight riding Fly and tidying up the yard. She tried Fly's saddle on Toad and found to her relief that it fitted, although she would have to buy a longer girth. The bridle let out enough to fit him too, just. But filling two hay-nets made her realize just how quickly two animals got through the food: it was imperative that she found a new home for Fly as soon as possible. She should have asked Mr. McNair in the morning. So full of Toad, she had clean forgotten her most important problem.

'I'll ring him up,' she decided.

But before she got round to it, he rang her. She was surprised.

'Ruth? I've got a proposition to put to you.' His hearty, domineering voice put her instantly on her guard. It was as if her instincts knew.

'This pony—Toadhill Flax—I hope you don't think it presumptuous of me, but I would like to make you an offer for him. Peter is quite set on having him back.'

'Oh.'

'I know you got him very cheaply, but I'd be quite happy to give you double—or anything in my own stables in exchange—that sort of size.'

'No.' She answered without hesitation.

'I beg your pardon?'

'I don't want to sell him.' It was almost as if he had made a physical assault on her. She felt breathless, almost hysterical.

There was a short silence. Then, sounding surprised, McNair said, 'There's no need to make your mind up quite so hastily. It's a very good offer, Ruth, and a very sensible one from your point of view. You stand to gain very substantially by it.'

He could only understand it from a dealing angle. He had no idea of her feelings at all. She could not bring herself to say anything.

'Are you still there?'

'Yes.'

'Would you like to come up here and talk it over? It's quite unnecessary to decide anything immediately. Perhaps come and see what we've got?'

She was silent.

Mr. McNair's voice softened, and became more confidential. 'It's not big business, Ruth. It's just that Peter's got this bee in his bonnet. It's Peter that wants him back. He always said I should never have sold him. If you remember it was round about when Toad went that Peter went off the rails, ran away and all that. There was always something special about that pony for Peter. He's asked me now—to talk to you about it. It seems to mean a great deal to him.'

34

'It means a great deal to me.'

'I can't hear you.'

No wonder. She found difficulty in speaking.

'Suppose you think about it, talk it over with your parents? And ring me back. Anything within reason, Ruth. I'm sure we can settle this amicably. I'll hear from you later, eh?'

Ruth put the receiver down.

'Who was that?' her mother asked. 'You look as if you've been struck by lightning.'

Ruth tried to compose her face. 'Only Mr. McNair. Nothing. About getting me some worm powders.'

Her brain was in complete confusion. She went upstairs and locked herself in the lavatory. Mr. McNair's proposition filled her with indignation; it was like being beaten over the head with reason, when reason was the very last thing that entered into her own relationship with the chestnut pony. No reason had entered into it yesterday when she had bought him, nor did it now. It was fate that had decided she should own that pony, and nothing Mr. McNair could say would persuade or influence her to change her mind. The force of her feelings was uncontrived. It was an instinctive reaction. She wanted no other pony at all, having become the owner of Toadhill Flax. He was all she had ever dreamed or desired. She knew that he could get her into the Pony Club team if she was good enough; he could take her out hunting, over any hunter trial course, and jump boldly in the show-ring. He was proved. If they were to fail, it would be her fault, not his. And having such complete confidence in him, she thought that it would prove a tremendous asset to her ambitions. It put all the onus on herself, and that was where she wanted it. She wasn't clever enough to train up a young pony. If she didn't have the integral confidence in the animal, she would never have the courage to attempt the whole business at all. Nobody else would understand how she felt. They all took it for granted; they had all this knowledge behind them, and parents to do all the worrying and make the decisions, and drive the horse-box and pay the entry-fees and say what went wrong and wait at the ring-side; but she had nothing, nothing at all save her pathetic ambition to join in. This was what Mrs. Meredith meant by saying her heart was in the right place. Right now her heart told her not to part with Toad at any price, not for two or three or even five times the amount she gave for him. But if she said all this to her mother and father they would call her a lunatic.

Perhaps she was.

She would ask Ted.

The problem wouldn't have been quite so acute if it hadn't been for Peter's part in it. She remembered Peter saying, a long time ago, that Toad was the only pony he had ever cared about. Underneath his hard-bitten, joky exterior she had always known there was another Peter lurking, the one that had once needed a psychiatrist to sort it out. She had seen it a few times, and sensed it often, but Peter was careful to pretend that nothing mattered very much. On the other hand, she couldn't help feeling that his present attitude was strangely possessive. If he had any feelings of affection for the pony, he ought to be very pleased that he had landed out of his hard times into such a loving new home. Even the professional McNairs wouldn't dispute that there was anything at fault with the care she lavished on her animals. Peter's actually wanting Toad again seemed to her more like a jealous obsession than anything else. She could not believe, and certainly didn't want to believe, that Peter needed Toad in any way; although she could see quite easily that Peter's life wasn't exactly lapped around with love and affection, his own mother having died some years ago, his father a hard man by nature and his new stepmother now taken up with a baby of her own. And yet his behaviour suggested this need—the way he had greeted Toad the evening before, even the abrupt way his voice had changed on the telephone when she had first mentioned the pony's name. Ruth, pondering, felt disturbed by these thoughts.

'But what about me?' She was a deserving case too. If Peter had his problems, nobody could say she had had an easy time with her horse-life. Right from the beginning, from buying Fly as an unbroken colt, and herself not even able to ride, it had been a struggle. She deserved Toad too.

She went downstairs again, very quiet and withdrawn. Whatever happened, her parents mustn't know about the offer. They would never allow her to refuse it. It was, in effect, a gift of a hundred pounds. Or, what she would have given her eyes for only the day before yesterday, the choice of any of the ponies in the McNair stable. There was no one she could discuss the matter with, even Ted. He would think she was potty if she refused. Or would he?

She realized she only wanted some one to agree with her, not really to discuss it at all. She decided to tell Ted; he knew Peter pretty well, and perhaps would see something in the whole business that eluded her understanding.

To see Ted without her parents' overhearing anything meant she had to waylay him putting his motor bike away, before he came indoors.

'Now what?' he said, switching off the engine and peering at her in the darkness. He knew her pretty well too, and recognized the signs. 'What's happened now?'

'The McNairs want me to sell Toad to them!' It burst out in an indignant wail. 'He's just rung up—offered me twice what we paid for him!'

'I say, whacko! That's luck if you like!'

'But I don't want to sell him!'

'Stone the crows, I might have guessed! Red rosette for perversity. I still don't see the problem, all the same. Refuse politely. Problem solved.'

'You think? I have refused and he's going to ring up again. Says I'm too hasty. If Mum and Dad hear, they won't let me refuse.' She repeated the gist of the conversation she had had with Mr. McNair.

'Go up the road to the call-box and say you've thought and no go.'

'I'd rather see Peter than Mr. McNair. Peter ought to understand why I don't want to sell him.'

'Peter wants him for the same reason you do. Emotional—you love him and all that rot. I would have thought Peter was beyond such childish whatevers.'

'That's what I thought. But if he isn't, it makes it dreadfully difficult. I owe them such a lot.'

'It's not all one way. You mustn't be a doormat. Tell you what. We could have a quick nip up to Peter's, and you can have a confrontation, while I have a look at their horse-box. It's got to go for its M.O.T. and old McNair asked me to have a dekko at its brakes. Good enough excuse anyway. Go and get a coat and your bonnet, and tell Mum. We'll be back in an hour.'

'Your dinner's ready.'

'It'll keep.'

After the inevitable skirmish about the dinner, they roared off to McNair's. Ruth felt nervous, and saw immediately that Peter was nervous too. He was in the feed-shed, measuring out feeds, and she came in through the doorway and saw his expression. He flushed up slightly, and went on with what he was doing.

'It's about Toad,' she said.

'Yes?' He put down the scoop and looked at her.

'Why do you want him back? You've got a whole stable to ride.'

'We've made you a good offer. You could have a pony worth three times as much if you want.'

'I want to know why.'

'He's a good pony.'

'Yes, but I want a good pony too. And that's not the reason. It can't be.'

'He's mine.'

'He was yours.'

'You know what I mean. You know perfectly well.'

Ruth knew exactly, with an awful plummeting of the heart, but could not accept it.

'But you wouldn't do anything with him now. You've always got to ride the others, you've no time.'

'I told you once—Toad is different. The only one.'

'You didn't have him for very long.'

'Long enough. He would do anything with me. You saw him. He won't do it for anyone else.'

'Oh, you're conceited!' Ruth burst out. The argument Peter was using was the very one she had no defence against. Peter, tough, larky Peter, showing a soft centre unnerved her completely.

'It's not conceit,' Peter said. 'You won't be able to ride him.'

'Why not?'

'He's too difficult.'

'I'm not a beginner any more!'

'What experience have you had? One overburdened nag with no pretensions to any form—how can you have learned enough to take on a pony like Toad? We just want to do you a favour.'

Flinging insults, Peter was not such a sympathetic character after all. Ruth felt strengthened.

'And suppose I want to take on a difficult pony? I know he can do it. Clever old you showed everybody, didn't you? You are just saying I can't ride him, to put me off. You want everything your own way.'

'There's no other animal I want.'

'And there's no other I want either!'

'Have it your own way. I just say that you'll find you can't manage him. And when that happens, we'll buy him off you.'

Ruth was incensed. Peter was his old mocking self, but now his mockery was not, as it always had been, funny and well-disposed but angry and vindictive. He was hurting Ruth on her most sensitive spot, her feeling of inadequacy in the face of the horsy professionals. She didn't believe that she wouldn't be able to ride Toad; she thought Peter was just saying it to make her sell. But he had taken the wrong tack. Perhaps he recognized this himself, for he then said:

'You are so stubborn! Nobody can talk to you when you don't want to hear! Good luck to you—that's all I can say!'

Ruth realized that there was nothing else she could say. Peter's face was cold and hard—rather like his father's could look at times —and Ruth sensed that his bitterness was final. He wasn't going to come down tomorrow and say that it had all been a joke. She didn't feel that there was anything that could easily be turned into a joke either.

'Everything went wrong,' she explained to Ted on the way home. 'I can't see him ever speaking to me again.'

'Oh, he'll come round. He's not a baby.'

No, Ruth thought. That was the trouble. He had looked formidably adult standing there by the feed-bins, and quite set in his determination to get the pony back.

'He's stubborn,' she said to Ted.

'Hark, who's talking!'

But with Peter turned into an enemy, Ruth was only just beginning to see the fresh problems that loomed ahead. She rather thought that her troubles were only just starting.

6

'LISTEN, Mummy, guess what? Ruth Hollis has bought Toadhill Flax.'

Jessica Meredith slipped down from her pony, Cuthbert, and peered into the loose box where her mother was unsaddling Florestan, her point-to-point horse. Mrs. Meredith came to the door and hung the saddle over the lower half.

'Ruth Hollis?'

'The girl with her heart in the right place,' Jonathan said.

'Good God,' said Mrs. Meredith. 'She's got Toad?'

'Yes, Eddie told me. We owe him another ten pence for Cuthbert. Steel's gone up again. He did removes in front and new behind.'

'Her heart will need to be in the right place if she's got Toad,' Mrs. Meredith said. 'Put the rugs on Florrie, Jonathan, will you? I'll pay Eddie when I go down. I'm starving for a coffee. Put Cuthbert away and come and tell me all, Jess.'

Mrs. Anstey, the housekeeper, had the coffee ready and waiting; Mrs. Meredith heaved off her boots and ran her hands through her frizzled hair. She was handsome more than pretty, with a very straight look which could be intimidating. Her children knew when to treat her with caution.

Mrs. Anstey set the cups out on the table and brought the coffee-pot and milk-jug.

'Bless you! My extremeties are quite frozen! And where did Ruth come across Toad then? I thought he'd gone from the area— I haven't set eyes on him since the McNairs sold him.'

'She bought him on the market for a hundred pounds,' Jessica said.

'A hundred! Good heavens, he must have come down in the world.'

'Eddie says he looks awful, all thin and droopy.'

'Does Peter know?'

'Eddie says Peter wants him back.'

'I should think so. I've never seen a pair quite like those two. It was magical what Peter did with him—right out of the rough and to the top in a matter of months. It was criminal of McNair to sell him. Peter was upset. I think it did him a lot of harm.'

'Well, if he wants him back now,' Jonathan said, 'he'll probably do a swap with Ruth. They'll find her a much more suitable animal, and everyone will be happy.'

'And my team!' Mrs. Meredith smiled happily. 'What a team we shall have! Peter and Toad, our Railway—that new girl with Bright Morning. I've found out that she's done really well with him. I rang her old D.C. and she said she's a goer.'

'And me,' Jessica put in.

'You're a bit young—fourteen. We'll see. Depends on how Cuthbert goes this year.'

'Oh, Mummy! You were talking about Ruth the other night, if she had a decent pony, and she's only fourteen.'

'We'll see. It's embarrassing having half the team in the family.'

'Jess only wants to be in the team if Peter's in it,' Jonathan said. 'It's nothing to do with the honour of the Pony Club.'

'Oh, shut up!' Jessica scowled at her brother.

'Don't tease, Jonathan. Who's that? Someone coming up the drive. Oh, heavens, I hope it's not that woman about the W.I. party. I'm supposed to have—'

'Unlikely. It's on a pony. Small and female.'

'Oh, someone for Jess.'

Jessica went to the window and peered out. 'It's not for me. It's Ruth Hollis and I don't know her, only by sight.'

'How odd.'

'Come to ask your advice, I expect. How to fatten a Toad to make it jump.' Jonathan flung open the kitchen door and shouted, 'Ahoy!'

'Oh, Jonathan, be sensible.' Mrs. Meredith went to the door. 'I can't come out. I haven't any shoes. What do you want?'

'I want to ask you—'

A freezing blast of wind roared across the yard straight into the kitchen. Mrs. Meredith said, 'Wait a minute! Jonathan, take her pony and she can come in for a moment. Put it in a box. Come inside a moment dear. Give your pony to Jonathan.'

'Come into my parlour said the spider to the fly.'

41

'Pardon?'

Ruth looked at Jonathan anxiously. 'I only wanted to ask about, if anyone wants to buy—'

'Come in, child. Quickly, before we're blown away.'

This wasn't what Ruth had wanted. She seemed fated to be overcome by situations outside her control. She had hoped to meet Mrs. Meredith out at exercise, say her piece and depart. The Meredith family on its home ground frightened her to death.

'My word, you look frozen. There's some coffee in the pot. Fetch another cup, Jess.'

Ruth, without exactly consciously looking, was aware of a beautiful room, very old, with enormous oak beams and a huge fire-place. But the heat now came from central heating, and the ancient ingle-nooks were filled with gleaming modern appliances, with enough dials for the pilot of a Jumbo Jet. It made a strange but marvellously comforting contrast, sitting at a scrubbed wooden table drinking delectable coffee out of an electric percolator—if only she hadn't so much to worry about. She couldn't believe that these people would understand her difficulties, even if she were to explain them in explicit detail, which she had no intention of doing. She merely hoped to get Fly sold, the most urgent of her considerations.

'I hear you've bought Toad, Peter's old pony,' Mrs. Meredith said.

'Yes. That's what I've come for really, to see if you know anybody who might like to buy Fly-by-Night.'

'I'll bear it in mind, dear. Everyone is asking in the spring. He's not really a beginner's, is he?'

'No.'

'He might not be too easy to place. Everyone wants a fool-proof pony, no tricks.'

'It's terribly urgent,' Ruth said, trying not to sound too desperate. 'I can't afford to keep two ponies, and I borrowed the money to buy Toad.'

'Oh dear, I do see. An advert in the local paper might be the best thing.'

Ruth, having hoped someone might have asked Mrs. Meredith if she knew of a pony like Fly, felt depressed. She had thought of that answer herself, without riding four miles for the suggestion.

'I just thought you might know of someone.'

'Not just at the moment. Won't Mr. McNair take him?'

Ruth hesitated. Jonathan had come back, which unnerved her, as she had never been within speaking distance of him before, and he was looking at her closely. Ruth was aware that she was very susceptible to Jonathan.

'It's a bit awkward,' she said. 'I don't like to ask him.'

'Whyever not? He often takes ponies to place, and he's a great friend of yours surely? I should think he would buy him off you if you asked him.'

Ruth didn't know what to say. She thought Mrs. Meredith, if she knew the story of her deadlock with Peter, would advise her to accept the McNair offer. And she didn't want that sort of advice.

'I've had a bit of an argument with Peter.' She had to say something as they were all looking at her.

'He wants Toad back, Eddie said,' Jessica put in.

'Yes.'

'Jess has just come back from Eddie's. I'm afraid there are no horsy secrets round here, as I'm sure you know,' Mrs. Meredith said. 'I take it you want to keep Toad? Is that what the argument is about?'

'Yes.'

'How do you get on with him?'

'I haven't ridden him yet. He's lame. Peter says he's very difficult and I won't be able to ride him.'

'That's a bit high-handed,' Mrs. Meredith said.

'I thought perhaps he just said it, because he wants him so badly.' Ruth found she had nothing to hide, the local grapevine having been working overtime.

'So badly? How strange. They were certainly a fantastic combination.'

'They belong together,' Jessica said.

'Oh, what twaddle,' Jonathan replied. 'Peter's got a whole stableful to ride. If Ruth found Toad on the market and had the guts to buy him, why on earth should she sell him on to Peter just because he asks?'

Ruth sent a glow of gratitude in Jonathan's direction. But Mrs. Meredith then spoilt it by saying to Ruth, 'I take it that if you let Peter have Toad back, McNair will offer you something good in exchange?'

Ruth nodded.

'There's a great deal in this business of the animal and the rider suiting each other. It's a very good offer. You would be able to try several and make up your mind at leisure. There's no doubt that there was an understanding between Peter and Toad. Whether you could get on as well with that pony as you might with another perhaps less highly-strung remains to be seen. It's a risk.'

'I knew it was a risk when I bought him. I wasn't even sure if it was Toad anyway, and not just some old dud.'

'And anyway,' Jonathan said, 'suppose she sells him back to Peter and Peter spends the whole summer winning everything with him, what will Ruth think then? That it could have been her? She'll never know whether she couldn't have done it too. You know perfectly well, Mother, that you just want Peter and Toad for your team, because they're a dead cert.'

'Jonathan, I wouldn't put the team before what's best for the individual rider.'

'Yes, you would,' Jonathan said. 'This particular individual rider doesn't want to be in the team at all, and you said it had to be whether it liked it or not.'

'Don't be ridiculous.' There was a note in Mrs. Meredith's voice which Ruth recognized as one of the ingredients of her reputation. Jonathan evidently recognized it too as he didn't pursue the argument. He switched rather cleverly.

'Peter has a new horse anyway. It can jump a house, according to him. So your team will be all right.'

'Really? Where did it come from?'

'Broke a girl's skull over in Northend and McNair got him almost for nothing. Name of Sirius.'

'I've heard of Sirius.'

'It's a nasty.'

'Poor Peter wouldn't have got him otherwise.'

'And anyway, if Ruth finds after a bit that Toad won't do it for her, presumably Peter would still have him back then, if he wants him so badly, and nothing would be lost. Except pride, of course.'

He said the last phrase as if he knew exactly what a large part it was likely to play in the tangled situation. Ruth sent another blessing winging in his direction—he understood. He smiled at her, and Ruth felt weak at the knees. He was lovely, in all respects. Her situation was just as black as it had been when she arrived, but she felt she had gained an ally. Not Mrs. Meredith particularly.

'I think you ought to think about it very carefully, dear. Wait till you can ride Toad out a few times, see how he goes. I'm only telling you what is sensible, nothing to do with any other considerations at all, in spite of what Jonathan says.'

'I think Peter ought to have Toad back if he wants him,' Jessica said, slightly belligerent.

'It's nothing to do with you, Jessica.'

Ruth felt older than Jessica, in spite of the fact that they were the same age. She felt that Jessica was quite childish, having had no troubles in her life to age her, as she had. She had a wide, incipiently beautiful face, with dark, direct eyes like her mother's beneath a black, squared-off fringe. She was a heroine type,

45

innocent and favoured and slightly spoilt. Ruth had the impression that Jonathan had perhaps suffered a little more, probably at the hands of his fierce mother; he was more hidden than Jessica; his eyes were more cautious. He had black hair like Jessica but, unlike hers, his curled closely in what Ruth thought was a quite delectable fashion, worn as long as no doubt Mrs. Meredith allowed. Ruth decided that she liked Jonathan very much.

She got up to go. Mrs. Meredith assured her she would let her know if she found a buyer for Fly, and Jonathan accompanied her across the yard.

'Is this your pony?' Ruth peered into the loose box next to where Fly was waiting, never able to resist looking at ponies. Railwayman had an enviable reputation, although Jonathan did not compete very much. At close quarters he looked very powerful, although not handsome: a dark strawberry-roan, clipped out to a nondescript mousy colour, with a hogged mane and a tail which looked as if a goat had been at it. He stood just under fifteen hands, and was a cobby type, with a slightly Roman nose and piggy eyes. He was much coarser than Toad, a cob deriving from draught blood, rather than, like Toad, a heavier, larger version of the lovely Welsh mountain pony.

'He's nothing to look at,' Jonathan said, unnecessarily. 'All right though,' he added loyally. 'I wouldn't swap.'

'Do you ride much in the winter?'

'Hunting, not much otherwise. I'm not all that keen—not to the exclusion of everything else. If I had to do him myself, I probably wouldn't. I'm too lazy.'

'I like the doing part,' Ruth said.

'Jess does too. Perhaps it's a female thing.'

'Could be. Like housework. Only girls aren't supposed to want to be like that any more, are they?'

'I like cooking,' Jonathan said. 'Not the cleaning-up though. This is Cuthbert—Jessica's. He's no great looker either. Florestan is the star round here for looks. That's Mother's.'

Cuthbert was a bay gelding, very honest and sensible-looking, about fourteen hands high. Florestan, the point-to-pointer, was a very dark bay, with brighter bits about the eyes and muzzle which gave him an old-painting look, Ruth thought—entirely beautiful with his classy thoroughbred blood stamping every inquisitive movement as he came over to meet the visitor.

'Do you ride him?' Ruth asked.

'Sometimes. He's got no tricks—just strong because he's so bursting full with good grub. Out of condition, he'd just be a quiet hack.'

Jonathan got Fly out for her and she mounted, somewhat reluctantly.

'The best of luck,' he said, meaningfully. 'You show 'em.'

'I hope so.'

She needed all the luck she could get. She had had no joy in her visit to the Merediths as far as her actual mission went, but talking to them had clarified the Toad situation somewhat. All the things Jonathan had said were exactly right: the visit had not been in vain.

7

RUTH put her advertisement in the local paper:

'Bay-roan New Forest gelding, 6 years old, 13.1 hands. Many rosettes jumping, gymkhana.' She did not say that the rosettes had been won against pretty potty opposition and were more for Musical Sacks than for under 13.2hh. jumping classes, but there were about fourteen pinned on the rail over her bed, if anyone demanded proof. On the Friday evening, the day the paper came out, she waited for the phone to start ringing in reply, but nothing happened. She sat on the stairs in the hall, staring at it. She guessed that Fly's going would be traumatic, but his staying would be even worse. She had had to borrow off Ted again for feed, and she had already discovered that Toad ate far more than Fly and she needed more money in any case. The paper-round, and two nights a week baby-sitting (Friday and Saturday were all her mother would allow, because of school the next day) were barely coping. Everything had happened at quite the wrong time of year. Summer would have been much more convenient.

Nobody rang.

The next morning, Ruth rode Toad for the first time. She shut Fly in the stable and took Toad out into the field. There was a suspicion of spring in the air, and plovers trundling over the grass as if on little wheels. Ruth, prepared for the very worst, mounted by the gate and sat looking at the unfamiliar blonde mane before her, feeling considerably farther from the ground than usual, altogether more strongly horsed. She did not know what to expect at all. The field was long and narrow, four acres altogether and well hedged all round with rampant hawthorn, some of which had strayed into the middle, along with several wild rose trees and spiky sloes. If Toad chose to take off, he could not go very far, although she could well be impaled in the process.

'Come, animal.' She squeezed him into a walk and he went unprotestingly, with a long easy stride. Quite different from Fly's short quick pace; she was amazed at the difference. She told herself that she ought only to walk and trot, but after she had walked and trotted without any excitement, she could not resist trying a canter down the length of the field. Toad went eagerly, with a mere shortening of the rein, faster than she would have wished, but it was so lovely that she was disinclined to be more prudent, and sat down enjoying it with a great leaping surge of the blood in her veins. It was a wonderful canter, smooth and powerful, enough to show her that owning Toad was quite the best thing that had ever happened to her, and that she was right to stick it out with him whatever happened. He pulled up satisfactorily at the end of the field, although not without showing her that it was more through goodwill on his part that he chose to stop rather than anything she was doing about it. Ruth had the first intimation of what a passenger she might feel if he chose to resist her: there was this fantastic feeling of dynamic strength, even with the animal so out of condition. Enough to be slightly frightening, to show her that Peter's words weren't entirely to put her off. And after the excitement of the canter, he would not settle again, but walked on sideways, pulling hard, lifting his feet up high as if he were on springs. It was exhausting, and made her hands and wrists ache; she wasn't used to such energy coming up into her body. She stopped him several times, not without difficulty, and got him to walk on with the reins relaxed, but only for a few paces. After that he would start jogging, bouncing up and down again, and the more she tried to hold him in, the more he pulled. After about half an hour she decided to call it a day.

'Next time I will only walk, and perhaps trot,' she thought. 'He was all right until we cantered. That's what set him off. I was too soon.'

But she was slightly worried. If it came to a battle of strength, it was quite obvious who was going to win. She could try and hold him back, but she knew that the solution did not lie in the rider using force: the more the rider used the more the horse used. One got nowhere. To overcome that particular problem required more riding skill than she possessed: a very firm and deep seat, powerful legs, tactful hands and complete confidence in one's ability.

She took him back to the stable thoughtfully. 'I shall need help,' she thought. And Peter wouldn't. She needed someone just to say, to give her courage. It was so difficult to work out things on one's own.

'But perhaps if I just ride him quietly every day, he will get used to me, and settle down.' Considering it was her first ride, it hadn't been bad at all. The mistake had been on her part, to canter. She should have been content with just walking. It all took so much time and patience! The slightly ominous factor in the incident was how strong he was in his thoroughly unfit state. If she fed him up and got him into condition . . . better not think about it. She decided she would ride him out quietly along the lanes, until she got to know him better. Most horses went more quietly along a road, rather than across acres of heady grass.

When she got back to the house, her father said someone had rung up for her.

'About Fly?'

'Yes. Said he was coming over to have a look at him.'

Half an hour later the phone rang again. Ruth answered. A very pleasant female voice said, 'I understand you have a pony for sale?'

'Oh, yes! Yes, I have.'

'Can you tell me something about him?'

'Oh, he's lovely! It's just that I've grown out of him. I've got another one you see. His name is Fly-by-Night. He's very good-looking, not heavy. Very good-natured, no nasty tricks at all. Perfectly sound. I've had him for three years and I've done all the Pony Club things with him. He's a good jumper, and he's fast.'

'Perhaps I could come and see him? Some time tomorrow?'

'Yes, of course. Somebody's coming today'—she thought she ought to get this in—'but tomorrow would be quite all right.'

'I'll bring my daughter. She's ten, but quite a good rider now, ready for something to take her on a bit. We've other horses but all too big for her as yet. I'll look forward to seeing you then.'

Ruth told her how to find the cottage, and rang off feeling highly optimistic. The woman's voice had suggested a gentle but efficient, farmish sort of woman; if she had a girl who could ride a bit, and lots of other horses, it would be a marvellous home for Fly, with lots of company and people who knew how to treat him. Ruth went into a dream, believing that her great difficulties were about to be solved, and that she would deliver Fly to a new, paradisical home in exchange for great wads of lovely desirable money, and have nothing to worry about ever again. But while she was thinking this, her father came into the hall and said, 'There's a large car in the drive and I think it might be the man who said he was coming to look at Fly. You'd better go out and be nice to him.'

She went out, and found a very large, red-faced man in a duffel coat looking dubiously down the orchard.

'This where the pony's for sale?' His voice was rough and brisk. Ruth looked at him closely, to see if he might be a suitable owner for Fly, and decided immediately that he wasn't. He looked to her a flash sort of man, more inclined to spend his money on cars and mock fur coats than pony-fodder. She guessed that he might have a spoilt little girl who was 'just crazy about ponies'.

'Yes,' she said. 'He's down in the field if you want to look at him.'

'Fine. It's not too muddy, I hope?'

'You needn't go in the mud.' He wore two-tone suede boots, she noticed, a generation too young for him. He had a tweed hat with a feather in the side and a large diamond ring. He was horrible.

She led him down the orchard, and he stood by the gate, on the bit that was still cobbled, and she went to catch Fly. He came eagerly, as always, and Ruth felt like a traitor, taking him into the yard to stand out for inspection by this flabby-faced, saggy-eyed man. Fly was so familiar; he was such a large part of her life that the thought of his going was almost impossible to dwell on. In her mind she desired to sell him very much for the most pressing of practical reasons, but in her heart she desired it so little that she realized that she had never let herself think about it at all up till now. Not the actual going. And now, when he stood at her shoulder and rubbed his head against her in his affectionate familiar way, she felt hot tears of remorse rising up inside her. She felt panic-stricken. Fortunately the man was looking at the pony, not at her, and Fly was standing quietly in an exemplary manner, as if he actually wanted to be sold to this horrible man, and the man smiled and said:

'Very nice. He might be just the thing. I've got a little girl that's just crazy about ponies, and it's her birthday next Saturday. She's kept on and on about a pony, and we've got a bit of land at the side, so I thought, well—if it'll make her happy—what are you asking?'

Ruth added twenty on to what she had decided and told him, but he didn't seem to be put off. So she said, 'Actually there's someone else who wants him. I would have to wait and decide with her first.'

'Okay, you do that,' the man said obligingly. 'I'll call you back later.'

Ruth put Fly back in the field and saw the man back to his car. After he had gone, she realized that she hadn't got his name and address; then she realized that she hadn't got the name and address of the nice-sounding woman either. She spent the rest of the week-end waiting for the woman to call, but she didn't, neither did she ring up. Ted said, 'It's the same as bikes. They say they'll call and you wait around for them, and they never turn up. Never let you know either.'

'But she must!'

'Don't you believe it.'

Ruth felt her familiar desperate feeling creeping over her again. Pride would not let her ask Mr. McNair to take Fly; Peter remained obstinately out of touch, and Ruth felt that she was not to be forgiven for the stand she had taken. Normally he rang up or came in and out several times a week, but since she had seen him at his place she had heard nothing of him. She missed him a lot. She felt friendless and in need of help. She remembered the girl at the auction, who had come to live at Hill Farm, and wondered if she had the nerve to ride up there and call, and see if they wanted to buy a thirteen-hand gelding. She decided she had. If she rode up quietly on Toad it would be good for him, and if her nerve failed her when she arrived at the gate she could always ride on past and no harm done. She was spurred on in this decision by a phone call from the man in the large car, saying he would be prepared to come down and pay her the cheque for Fly if he was still for sale. She knew that she ought to be overjoyed by this news, but she felt miserable and unworthy and utterly depressed. She went out straight away and groomed and saddled Toad and set out for Hill Farm, leaving Fly whinnying sadly at the gate.

The whinnying was pathetic, so obviously saying, 'Don't leave me,' and Ruth was torn. She wanted to enjoy Toad, who was behaving in an exemplary manner, but all she could think of was Fly going to a home where he would be treated like a new toy by a nasty spoilt child and neglected by the ignorant parents. She arrived at Hill Farm without having made her mind up about anything, and saw the girl Thea going in at the gate on a bicycle.

There was no need to have any nerve at all, for Thea said, 'Oh, hullo, are you Ruth Hollis?'

'Yes.'

'I'm supposed to have met you. The Pony Club woman said.'

'Mrs. Meredith?'

'Yes. She said you'd bought a wild horse and needed moral support. Is that it?'

'Did she really say that?'

'No, not exactly. I'm sorry. Tact isn't my great thing. She said you lived near and if I was new I ought to look you up all friendly-like, and she hoped we might both come to a team practice some time, as soon as the ground dried up a bit. And you had a very good new pony but lacked confidence.'

'Oh. She said I lacked confidence?'

'Yes. I shouldn't have said that either, should I?'

'Well, it's true. I more or less told her that myself. I know he can do it, but I'm not sure if I can.'

'That's not lacking confidence, that's just being sensibly modest. Better that way round than assuming because you've bought a good pony you're going to go straight out and win everything. If it was that easy, everyone would do it.'

'Yes.' Ruth decided she liked Thea. She seemed very grown-up for sixteen, not in a sophisticated way, but in a responsible, sensible sort of way. 'It used to belong to Peter McNair. It did everything with him.'

'Oh, *him*,' Thea said, wrinkling her nose. 'Well, it would with *him*, wouldn't it?'

'Don't you like him?' Ruth asked hopefully.

'So stuck-up. Superior. Stand-offish. Conceited.'

Ruth considered these descriptions with interest. Peter wasn't any of those things at all, but was often credited with them, mainly by his fellow-competitors. She had been a fellow-competitor with him herself a few times, and knew that his distant, pre-occupied manner was due to concentration, often with a difficult pony, and with his pure professionalism. He only entered to win, not to have a fun day. Or, if not to win, to show a pony to its best advantage, with prospective buyers in view. It was his upbringing. He couldn't help it.

She smiled. 'He's all right really.'

It was easy to talk to Thea. She found herself telling her how

54

and why she had fallen out with Peter, and Thea asked her to
come and see Bright Morning.

'In fact, I was going to take him out. If you're out for a ride,
would you mind if I came with you?'

'No. Of course not.'

'I've got to go over to the McNairs', actually. We bought a
horse-trailer off them and mother says its lights don't work and
has given me the job of complaining. After all you've said, could
you bear calling on them?'

Ruth considered it. There was just the chance that, if she found
Peter in a good mood, the stupid quarrel would be finished and
Mr. McNair would have Fly and all her troubles would be over.
It was worth trying, although she was not optimistic, and her
instincts didn't want to go at all. Toad would probably choose to
buck her off in the McNair yard and Peter would laugh unkindly.

'Ted could mend your trailer lights,' she said hopefully. 'He's
my brother.'

Thea's face darkened momentarily and she said abruptly, 'No.
I'd rather go to McNair's. It's his pigeon.'

Thea saddled Bright Morning and led him out. Ruth saw immediately that he was in a different class from the usual Pony
Club beast, a dark chestnut Anglo-Arab with flashy white stockings
standing about fourteen and a half hands. He had a fine dark red
mane and tail and a narrow white stripe down his nose, and was
edgy and fidgeting, making Thea swear as she tried to tighten his
girths. He made Toad look like a cart-horse. As soon as Thea
mounted Ruth could see that she was more than competent. She
looked very strong in the saddle—possibly too strong as far as her
hands were concerned, although the pony only wore a snaffle.
Ruth compared everybody's riding to Peter's; he never appeared
to be doing anything at all, which was her criterion. Thea certainly
appeared to be trying hard to make Bright Morning walk in a
straight line down the drive, but as she was succeeding beautifully,
Ruth was impressed. Toad followed fairly bouncily, but not
enough to cast doubts.

'They make a nice pair,' Thea said, when they were side by
side in the lane. It was true, the two chestnuts shining brightly
against the sombre winter hedges and the wet plough, turned
and gleaming to the horizon. The air was heavy with English
winter damp, the moisture gathered on every twig, webbing the

grass; the sky pearl-grey and constant and still. Ruth accepted it happily, but Thea said, 'Ugh, this weather!' She was a natural protester, Ruth sensed; not a moaner, but one of life's fighters, improvers.

'How long have you had Bright Morning?'

'Two years—bit more. My father bought him for me.'

'Does he ride?'

'He's dead. He did, yes.'

Ruth felt embarrassed, remembering that she had known there was no father. She wanted to ask what had happened to him, but didn't like to. However, Thea said, 'He was killed in a car accident on the motorway last year. Him and my brother Mick. Mick was eighteen. It wasn't their fault at all—that's what's so unfair. It takes a lot of getting used to, them not being there.'

There wasn't any reply to a statement like that. Ruth could only accept it as a personal rebuke—she thought *she* had troubles! It put everything into grim perspective, reminding her in a flash of the day—in fact, about the same time ago—when Ted was nearly killed on his motor bike. But nearly was different. Ted had been as good as new six months later. She remembered vividly the shock even now, the sudden desperate moment when you no longer took a brother for granted. She realized that Thea's tough manner probably covered up a whole lot of gaping pits in her life-history, the sort one would not want to gaze into ever again.

'Having so much to do is a good thing,' Thea said. 'Moving and everything—it helps. And the animals—there's never any time to sit around. There never was actually, but we thought we'd keep it that way. That's why we bought the trailer, so we can still go to shows in the summer, and hunting and everything. We had a big box before, but it needed a Heavy Goods Licence, so we sold it and got the trailer instead. We shall run out of money, of course, but Mother says we'll bother about that when it happens. She's like that. No sense of responsibility.' Thea smiled broadly. 'It's better that way really. If she just sat and cried and worried it would be awful. I worry far more than she does, but it works all right. She wants to buy some more horses, a good brood mare. But she gets carried away.'

'She wanted to buy Toad.'

'Yes, she did. I thought that was him, when you rode up. I was trying to think where I'd seen him before. He was a bargain really.

If we'd realized he was Peter McNair's ex-nag, we would have bought him. She was right, you see, and I put her off.'

'Well, I'm glad,' Ruth said. 'Else I wouldn't have got him.'

'She's got an eye for animals.'

That was the remark that Ruth had remembered. Life was odd, she thought affectionately—like a complicated Fair Isle knitting pattern, with the same bits and colours recurring, large patches of plain knitting and then a lot of intricate bits all woven in together. Toad was a very complicated bit of pattern, which she was not sure she would be able to master.

They reached the McNair establishment without incident and turned into the long gravel drive with its beautiful post and rail fences on either side. Ruth now felt distinctly unhappy, and said to Thea, 'I'll wait at the gate at the top, and not come into the yard. I don't particularly want to see Peter.'

'Okay. I'll only be a minute,' Thea said.

But when they got to the top of the drive there was no sign of either Mr. McNair or Peter in the yard, only harmless friendly Maggie the groom, and old George unloading hay into the barn, so Ruth rode in behind Thea.

'They're both in the field, giving Sirius a going-over,' Maggie said.

The temptation was too much for Ruth. They rode out of the far side of the yard down the little lane which led to the schooling-field and pulled up by the hedge where they could see what was going on. Ruth was agog to see the notorious Sirius, if not Peter.

Mr. McNair was in the field, watching Peter as he rode down a line of six cavalettis at a slow canter. The pony was a dark brown thoroughbred type with a narrow white blaze, beautifully proportioned and with what looked to Ruth the impulsion of a jet-plane. He jumped in enormous bounds, as if he found it impossible to consider anything as lowly as a cavaletti two feet high and, although the jumps were generously wide apart for the exercise, he went down the row without any strides in between at all.

'God Almighty! Take him slower!' Mr. McNair bawled at Peter, who turned and came back to the top of the field again at a belting trot. Up by the hedge he brought Sirius to a standstill, and Ruth felt that he must have seen them through the bare twigs, but he made no acknowledgement. He had his hands full, it was evident at close quarters, and as soon as he turned towards the line

of cavalettis again Sirius broke into his great bounds. With anyone
else Ruth felt that he would have got completely out of control but
Peter managed to keep him straight and got him down the line of
jumps, not at a trot, but at a much slower canter than the time
before. Ruth, realizing that this might prove to be her own problem
with Toad—too much excitement when faced with jumps—tried
to see how it was done but, as usual with Peter, nothing showed.
He sat very still, kept his hands very still and his legs appeared to
do nothing at all, but Ruth knew that the appearance was an
illusion. It was pure skill and beautiful to watch.

Mr. McNair didn't appear to think so as he shouted out, 'A trot
I said! Who's the bloody boss?'

Peter did it again and again, and each time Sirius accepted his
lot with better grace, until he was trotting steadily, beautifully
balanced, down the row of poles. Ruth wondered if she was
capable of achieving such an improvement in Toad in so short a
time, and knew she wasn't.

'All right. See if he'll take the big ones more quietly now. Just
once and then he can go in.'

The big ones were two fences of poles about four feet high in
the middle of the field. Peter went down to the bottom and turned
Sirius towards the first one. Immediately he started tearing away
like a train, but Peter frustrated him by making him circle several
times first, until he was more collected. But when he brought him
round to jump again the pony seemed to go mad with excitement,
all his lessons forgotten. Peter let him go, whether by intention or
whether because he could not stop him Ruth could not tell, and
Sirius tore at the jump and jumped it with about two feet to spare,
big as it was. Peter, unprepared for the generosity of Sirius' effort,
was slightly unbalanced and let the reins run out through his
fingers so as not to jab him in the mouth, and Sirius unkindly
took advantage of this unexpected freedom and, before Peter could
gather himself together again, was off at a tearing gallop for the
next fence.

'He's bolting,' Thea said.

Ruth wasn't sure. There wasn't much time to turn the pony
away safely, the jumps being fairly close together, and she guessed
that Peter had decided it was safer to jump. She saw him take an almighty pull at the pony to try and steady him. Sirius shortened his
stride and jumped beautifully, again with feet to spare. Peter was

ready for him and holding him in to steady him immediately he landed, but Sirius was too strong for him.

'Yes,' Ruth said. 'He is.'

She had never seen a full-scale bolt before. She had been run away with plenty of times herself, but never truly bolted with, the pony completely set in its intention to gallop itself to a standstill. The field was not very big, not big enough for the present circumstances, and the pony's thundering blind gallop was terrifying to watch. It was utterly lacking in any sort of predictable motive, like a madness, the eyes wild, the action jolting, swerving, ungoverned.

'God! Rather him than me!' Thea said briefly.

Peter appeared to be sitting there without trying to stop him, probably having decided to concentrate on steering. His father was waving his arms about and shouting instructions, but Ruth did not see much point in this. She thought that Peter must be wholly occupied with his problem to the exclusion of anything his father might be saying and—if he was merely human, which she knew he was—pretty frightened. It was a matter of getting out of the situation in one piece. He went round the field twice, keeping the pony out of trouble, and by the third circuit he had got the reins crossed over the pony's neck and was managing to slow down somewhat. Sirius came pounding towards the hedge. The ground was wet and slippery and so far Peter had avoided any sharp turns by his clever steering. But now, at last managing to slow down, he judged that the hedge would stop Sirius. Sirius saw it and swerved, lost his footing and almost came down, dropping one shoulder sufficiently to send Peter shooting over his head. Peter flew through the air and came up hard against the foot of the gate-post close to where Ruth and Thea were watching. Sirius carried on down the field and Mr. McNair ran out waving his arms.

Ruth looked at Peter, rolling about in the grass making groaning, winded noises, and realized that she had put herself in the worst possible position for any hope of patching up their quarrel. She had left it too late to ride quietly and inconspicuously away. When Peter got up and leaned painfully over the gate he saw Toad and Bright Morning standing there, agog at the goings-on, and Ruth and Thea regarding him uncertainly.

'Are you all right?' Thea asked.

Peter straightened up abruptly, glowered at Ruth and said shortly, 'Yes, of course.' He hadn't enough breath to say anything else. Mr. McNair, having caught Sirius, came towards them, muttering and blaspheming.

'A bullet, that's what it needs. That woman was right, for once. I should have listened. We'll get rid of it, Peter. It's not worth the trouble. Good morning, girls. Have you come to swap Toad, Ruth? Fancy this one?'

Ruth, watching Peter at that moment, saw him dart her a look of pure incredulity. It was, for one fleeting moment, full of hope and excitement. Afterwards she told herself she had imagined it, that it was something she had both dreaded and expected, and therefore she saw it, but, at the time—shocked at the misunderstanding—she almost cried out, 'Oh, no! No. I just came up with Thea. Not about ponies at all.'

'You're not offering us a price for Sirius then?' Mr. McNair asked. 'No takers? I'm afraid he's only fit for pet-food. Put him away, Peter.'

Peter's face, quite closed-down again, mud-splashed and angry, turned to Sirius and he reached out for the reins.

'No,' he said. 'It's no good putting him away now. I'll have to go on with him.'

'It's not worth it, Peter. He's dangerous. A bullet is all he's good for.'

'No,' Peter said. 'Not with a jump like that. He could go to Wembley next year.'

'They'd love it—an exhibition like we've just seen,' Mr. McNair said grimly.

'Well, give him a bit longer. He'll settle.'

'It's your neck.'

'Sirius, you fool.' Peter put the reins back over the pony's neck, and stroked him slowly behind the ears. 'You fool horse. You're frightened for nothing.'

The pony was marvellous-looking, its nostrils opened out and red, its eyes round and wild. Ruth wouldn't have mounted it for a hundred pounds. Its coat curled with sweat, shining dark with slight golden mottles showing signs of its summer brightness. Mr. McNair held him and Peter mounted again. The pony swung about, afraid, its flanks heaving. Mr. McNair looked worried.

'Just steady then.'

'Just walking,' Peter agreed.

He rode away down the field, talking to the pony. Even Ruth, who took Peter for granted, was impressed by his forgiving nature and dedicated patience. It was hard to forgive an animal so readily when it tried to kill you like that. Mr. McNair watched him go and then turned back to the girls with a shrug. They turned their ponies and walked back up to the yard with him.

'What's wrong with him?' Thea asked. 'He's been frightened?'

'Yes. Stupid handling. He's a splendid natural jumper. He was well broken in and jumped well in the ring as a youngster. Then some morons got him, just to win, couldn't ride—he's very spirited —they clamped down on him, beat him about because he wouldn't do it—he didn't know what they wanted. Now, as soon as he starts jumping again he remembers all the trouble he got into before and goes potty. Not the first time it's happened and won't be the last, I'm afraid.'

'Peter's very patient,' Thea said.

'He likes him for some reason,' McNair said. He looked at Ruth and said, 'Not changed your mind about Toad, you say?'

'No, I'm afraid not,' Ruth said, feeling dreadful.

'Pity,' Mr. McNair said.

Ruth opened her mouth to pursue this dangerous conversation, then thought better of it. She just couldn't understand Peter's attitude. Perhaps Mr. McNair sensed this, for he said, half apologetically, 'Peter's a funny boy. Don't worry about it, Ruth. I must admit there was a bond between the two of them—it's amazing what that pony would do for Peter, even when it was half wild straight off the hills. But I'm no sentimentalist. I think Peter's harking back, and there's no good in that. Perhaps with all that work to do on Sirius, he'll stop bothering.'

Afterwards Thea said, 'It's like a teddy-bear or something.'

'Whatever do you mean?'

'Peter wanting Toad. It doesn't make sense any more. Not when you've got a beauty like Sirius—if he stops bolting, that is.'

'He does want him though. It makes me feel awful.'

'He'll grow out of it. Don't worry! He's got enough on his plate with that animal he's got now. I must say, I couldn't do what he does. I thought Morning was bad enough, early on, but I never had Peter's sort of patience.'

It was very rare, Ruth agreed. She didn't know anybody else who had this thing with horses like Peter had: the way he turned to them, away from humans, as if he preferred the equine race altogether. The way he had ridden off down the field, prepared to go through the whole thing again . . . he was, in fact, still riding slowly round the schooling-field when they left an hour later. Ruth wasn't sure whether it was pure dedication, or whether he was waiting until she had gone. She did miss his friendship badly and wondered whether it was gone for ever. Coming face to face with him again under the present circumstances, just after he had been ignominiously thrown, had been unfortunate, and he had made no indication that he wanted to be friendly again.

'Of course, if you do well with Toad, Peter will be terribly jealous,' Thea said, not helping anything at all.

'And if I don't—' Ruth said. It seemed there was no joy either way.

Thea laughed, which improved things. Ruth remembered that it was all supposed to be fun, and felt quite a bit better.

Before they parted Thea said, 'If you want to bring Toad up to our place for a bit of schooling we've got some quite decent jumps.' The morning, having failed in its initial purpose, had borne fruit in other directions, just like her visit to the Merediths. Ruth rode home feeling moderately optimistic.

8

THAT evening the man with the two-tone boots brought a cheque and a horse-trailer and took Fly away. Ruth, having led Fly into the trailer and tied him up, fled back to the house, locked herself in her bedroom, put the pillow over her head and cried and cried. It was no good trying to remind herself that it was all for the best; she had done what she wanted; that she was very lucky. Reason did not prevail. She cried herself stupid. Her mother was quite sympathetic and came up with a cup of coffee and said, 'Come on, dafty, it's not the end of the world. There's a good show on the box. Dry your eyes and come down.'

Ruth told herself that it could have been her father and her brother disappeared for ever, like poor Thea; but even that didn't make any difference, Ted that evening being perverse and gloomy after an argument with his Barbara and her father in no way as lovable as Fly. One's imagination just couldn't stretch to removing one's father from the scene. That it had happened to Thea—and to Peter too, except that it had been his mother—made no difference. But Fly, darling Fly, gone to a dubious fate . . . if only it had been the farm lady with the nice voice or somebody more sympathetic. Ruth was plagued with remorse and watched the television through a blur of tears, kindly ignored by her family. Ted got his loan back and Ruth had enough money left over to see Toad in feed until the summer grass.

When she went back to school after the Christmas holidays she found Peter unapproachable. He wasn't in her class fortunately but in the one above, so she didn't see much of him, but they had talked in break before, or in the lunch-hour. Now he avoided her. But as if in compensation Thea, new and friendless in the O-level year, came and talked horse instead, and at the week-ends Ruth rode up to Hill Farm to school Toad. With Thea for moral support, Ruth found that she could contemplate her difficulties with rather more equanimity. For there were difficulties, and Peter's threats were not proved empty.

As Toad got fitter, which he did very quickly, he became much stronger to ride. He was all right at slower paces, and had no nasty tricks or vices at all, but once into a canter he wanted to keep on going and, faced with jumps, he could not wait to get at them, tearing away like Sirius himself.

Unlike Sirius, his dash was due purely to his own exuberant spirit, not to fear, but Ruth lacked the experience to exert the firm authority that was required. All she could do was exert her own strength against Toad's, and hers ran out long before his did. After a mere ten minutes she would be exhausted, arms and shoulders numb, and blisters raw in the palms of her hands, and Toad would be dancing about as if on gigantic springs—if she held him from going forward he merely went up and down instead like a yo-yo. She could not physically continue.

'It's a boy's pony,' Thea's mother said once, when she didn't know Ruth was in earshot. 'Such a strong ride, and she's such a slender thing.' Ruth felt as if a guillotine had fallen across her neck.

'Look, I must!' she said to Thea. 'I just can't not—'

'There's no question of not,' Thea said scathingly. 'You've just got to improve, you twit. There's nothing wrong with him.'

'Just me?'

'In a nutshell'—more kindly.

But even Thea found him a handful. They tried him in various bits, but he went best in a snaffle with a dropped noseband. Any sort of curb made him worse.

'Lots of steady work in a confined space,' Mrs. Parker said in her lovely vague way.

'When?' Ruth asked crossly. There were only week-ends, until the evenings got longer, and even when they did there was always deadly homework.

Peter McNair was reputed to work Sirius every day before school, getting up at six o'clock, but Ruth found it impossible. Sirius was kept in, and was clean and lovely when Peter went to saddle him at six o'clock, unlike Toad, out in the field and caked with mud. Ruth only brought him in if the weather was bad, not wanting to spend money on straw.

Even so, very slowly, she found that she was improving, her leg muscles and seat growing stronger. She felt safer, and her confidence improved. Thea's moral support was enormously helpful.

'Even if he's not improving, you are,' she said bluntly. 'One day he'll get the message. Morning was pretty awful when I first had him. Of course, he still is,' she added. 'But not all the time.'

Bright Morning, Ruth discovered, was an unpredictable animal, more like a mare than a gelding. Sometimes he would and sometimes he wouldn't. He was given to standing on his hind legs if he felt out of sorts. At least Toad was consistent, and always wanted to go. He never refused, but often knocked jumps down because he was out of control and going too fast. He had never knocked them down with Peter.

At the beginning of March Ruth received a letter from Mrs. Meredith inviting her to 'a schooling morning for possible team members and those wishing to take B test in the summer'. Ruth wasn't sure which heading she came under, but as she was too young to take B test until next year she could only imagine it was the first. She was terrified of exhibiting how little control she had over Toad in public, but Thea said, 'That's what it's for, isn't it? To help you? Sort you out. The more of this you can get the better.'

Ruth had to admit that Thea was right. Also that she had committed herself to this course knowing perfectly well what she was doing. If she had just wanted to hack about she would never have bought Toad anyway. But the first public admission of her impossible ambitions embarrassed her: more so as she was pretty sure Peter would be there to see how right he had been. But there could be no climbing down now.

The night before the meeting Ruth shut Toad in and groomed him thoroughly and washed his mane and tail. At least he would be a credit to her in appearance if not in manners. He looked a different pony now from the one in the market, having lost his hang-dog, head-down resignation, and put flesh on over his ribs and flanks. When a good deal of his winter coat had been brushed out and his summer coat shone through smoothly, the colour of new copper, his white mane gleaming, he looked to Ruth highly desirable. He was friendly and kind, lipping gently at her hand for a titbit, not missing Peter at all. She stood there for some time talking to him, wishing she was as good as he was, wondering how it would all work out. She often wished she didn't want so much, that she could be a happy failure, but it wasn't in her nature. Her family was always telling her she took everything too seriously, but she couldn't help how she was. She had a low opinion of what she considered her failings, and wished that she was as tough and brave as Thea who had far more to worry about than she had, but didn't. Thea never thought of the traps and pits, only the plain simple path ahead, an overburdened but optimistic girl. Ruth tried to think optimistically, and remembered how nice Jonathan was and that tomorrow, with luck, he would be there. Much cheered, she went to have a bath and wash from herself the dirt that she had just transferred from Toad.

Jonathan was there, but obviously under obligation, not from inclination. When Ruth and Thea rode into the Meredith yard, ten minutes early, they overheard a sharp exchange between the D.C. and her son outside Railwayman's loose box and Jonathan, in old jeans and T shirt, was dispatched abruptly to the house. Mrs. Meredith's expression changed from the familiar one of parental displeasure to a polite welcoming one when she saw the girls, and she came over and said, 'How nice your ponies look! I'm so glad you were able to come. I wanted to get this in before the first proper rally in the holidays, as it's easier to cope when the whole herd isn't here. I would have done it earlier, only the ground has been so wet. There should be about eight of you today, so we should be able to get some good work done. How's Toad going for you, Ruth?'

Ruth hesitated and Thea said firmly, 'Very well.'

Ruth was surprised and grateful.

'Splendid!' Mrs. Meredith left them to go and meet Mr. McNair who was driving the McNair trailer into the yard, and presently Jonathan reappeared dressed in proper riding clothes and looking fed up. He got Railwayman out of his box and gave the girths another heave without saying anything. The pony looked magnificently fit, gleaming and hard in what Ruth thought of as really professional condition. Ugly as he was, he had a strangely powerful presence which compelled admiration. Ruth could understand why Jonathan had said he wouldn't swap him.

Mrs. Meredith came back and said acidly to Jonathan, 'Your *hat*, Jonathan.'

'I can't find it.'

'It's in the tack-room. Go and fetch it.'

She held Railwayman and Jonathan fetched his hat and crammed it on mutinously. He mounted and his mother said, 'Take the girls on down to the field. Jessica and David are already down there. There's just Jane and Martin still to come.'

Ruth and Thea followed Jonathan through the yard gate and across a lane into another field laid out with markers and jumps. They pulled up inside the field and Jonathan said, 'You two are riding with me and Peter. Mother's taking us. I refused to go in the other ride with that old goat Milburn in charge. It's bad enough having your own mother, but worse with him.'

'Oh, he's ghastly. I know him,' Thea said.

'We were supposed to have Gary Major—he's all right. In fact he's super. But he's got hung up with his wife in hospital or something and rang to say he couldn't come. And old Milburn was all we could get at short notice.'

'He bawls at you,' Thea said.

'But he doesn't *know*—'

'He thinks he's still in the cavalry,' Jonathan said. 'All grip and guts. He was all right seventy years ago. Have you heard Peter take him off?'

At this moment this promising conversation was cut short by Mrs. Meredith arriving in her Range-Rover with the 'old goat' Milburn beside her, an elderly gentleman in riding boots and a flat cap with what Ruth thought of as a whisky face. She was glad she was getting Mrs. Meredith and not him. Peter followed to complete their ride on an impeccably turned-out Sirius. He nodded at Thea, ignored Ruth, and started to talk to Jonathan. Ruth decided she hated him. She dreaded Toad showing her up in front of Peter. Sirius appeared to be perfectly quiet and well-mannered. Of course, Ruth thought bitterly.

Mrs. Meredith took Milburn down the field and introduced him to his pupils and came back and told them to get warmed up, walking and trotting round the marked-out track. Jonathan led and Ruth made sure she got behind Peter so that he wouldn't be able to watch her. Toad felt like dynamite as soon as they started trotting, lifting his forelegs up high with impatience, but Sirius went smoothly, like a show-hack.

'Relax, Ruth!' shouted Mrs. Meredith. 'Don't lean forward. Relax your hands.'

Her nervous clamp was driving Toad mad. She relaxed, and Toad barged forward into Sirius's quarters. Sirius lashed out and Peter gave him a belt for kicking, and Sirius started to do his wild gliding trot, faster and faster. Toad followed, breaking into a canter. Mrs. Meredith screamed at them:

'Steady on! It's not a circus! Come back!'

Ruth heaved Toad round by sheer brute strength and came to a hot, tussled halt in the centre of Mrs. Meredith's school. Peter came back smoothly and halted beside her, but Sirius had lost his composure and would not stand still, fidgeting and backing.

'Hm, not a very good start. Get behind Railwayman, Peter, and you behind Thea, Ruth, and let's just walk, shall we? Try not to tense up, Ruth. Let him go up outside Thea if it helps.'

She looked as if she was trying hard not to be irritated, and Ruth didn't feel she could blame her. Peter looked cross too. They started off again. Ruth was pretty sure that Mrs. Meredith had been in a bad temper before they started—something to do with Jonathan —and was not in the mood to be patient. Her bad luck, Ruth thought.

Toad didn't actually run away with her, and she managed to keep him in his place through the schooling, but the effort exhausted her. The other three behaved in exemplary fashion, even Sirius, and Ruth hoped that perhaps Toad didn't look as bad as he felt. At least Mrs. Meredith didn't shout at her. And if one wanted to be optimistic, one could always admit that Toad was right up to his bit and moving freely with plenty of impulsion, highly desirable qualities. Perhaps Mrs. Meredith *did* think that. Ruth could only hope for the best.

Mrs. Meredith called them into the middle and said, 'You'll have to remember, if we're aiming at an Area Trials team, that the dressage section counts for a good deal. It's no good just relying on jumping to get you through. I can't say I'm impressed so far, but I think we have the material. Put it that way. We'll try some jumping now—nothing too ambitious, and then we'll work out some sort of a training programme, in light of what's wanted. I know your feelings about these trials—as long as you can bat round the cross-country course at a rate of knots and end up in one piece you think you've done everything that matters. Well, there's more to it than that—although I grant you, it's no good taking on an animal for its pretty manners if it hasn't got the courage and the steam for the cross-country. I don't think we're lacking there, in fact I think we're extraordinarily lucky this year to have four such proved contenders—' Ruth wasn't sure if she was imagining it, but she thought Mrs. Meredith's glance flashed doubtfully in her direction when she said this. She remembered one of the instructors last year saying to the D.C., 'The child needs guts to do the Area Trials. The courses are pretty stiff. The standard is going up all the time.' Jonathan, Thea and Peter had all done it before, once. Thea said she had had one refusal and three knock-downs. This was the previous year, when she had been riding for her old Pony Club. Jonathan had gone clear on Railwayman and Peter had had two knock-downs with a pony that had been sold immediately afterwards. What they had all done in the dressage and show-jumping sections, Ruth had no idea.

'Come on, now. Go down the cavaletti and over the bars, one at a time. Peter first, the others follow on.'

Ruth had to concentrate, and had no eyes for the others. She hoped to follow Thea close enough to please Toad, who was tearing to go, but Mrs. Meredith shouted out, 'Wait a moment, Ruth, not too close!' and she had to take an almighty pull to stop Toad going too fast. They were just coming to the first cavaletti, and Toad did his yo-yo act in front of it, then took off with a wild plunge and landed squarely on the bar with his hind-legs, breaking it in half. Ruth, jolted half out of the saddle, had no time to steady him for the next one, which he knocked over in his excitement but fortunately did not demolish. The next one he cleared, but by the time he got to the bars he was going so fast that he knocked them flying. Ruth heard the hollow booming noise of falling poles behind her like the tolling of a funeral bell; she turned Toad in a large, wild circle, in no hurry to face Mrs. Meredith again, and certainly not Peter. Jonathan grinned at her. Mrs. Meredith was heaving aside the broken cavaletti, trying not to look as if it mattered.

'Not very good,' she called out. 'Let's have you one at a time. Peter!'

Sirius was pulling like a train but Peter got him to jump beautifully, placing him exactly right at every obstacle. This was what Ruth knew she couldn't do, trying so hard merely not to fall off or be run away with. The jumps came at her quite arbitrarily, in the middle of all the fuss and bother, and she had to leave it completely to Toad to either jump them or knock them down. When it was her turn again, the performance was much as before, only Toad ran out at the poles this time, and Ruth, unprepared, very nearly fell off. This was dreadful, and quite unexpected. She brought him back and faced him at the poles again. This time he jumped them but knocked the top one down. Afterwards, Ruth had a hard job to stop him, and disappeared half-way down the field before she could get him together again. When she came back, wishing she was dead, Mrs. Meredith came over to her and said, 'I didn't realize he was quite such a handful. Slip off him a moment, dear, and let me see you ride Bright Morning. Thea is going to try Railwayman. You all need practice on other horses, especially if you're going to take your B test. Come on, Thea.'

Ruth got up on Bright Morning and shortened her stirrup a hole. She wasn't sure what was in Mrs. Meredith's mind, but was glad to have her own thoughts diverted. She had ridden Bright Morning before, at Thea's, and liked him. Strangely enough, he needed pressing on into his jumps, a great change from her usual experience. She rode him towards the jumps, and his smooth canter broke out beneath her. She felt quite calm and happy, and he jumped perfectly for her, and pulled up obediently afterwards. Ruth felt a lot better.

'Very good!' Mrs. Meredith beamed at her.

Thea set off on Railwayman, looking worried. Railwayman looked quite different for her, and jumped badly, dropping his hocks and knocking the top pole off.

'The old devil,' Mrs. Meredith said. 'Take him again, Thea! Drive him on with your legs!' To Ruth she said, 'He takes advantage. He's very much a one-man horse.'

Thea, annoyed, rode him strongly at the poles, and the cob jumped well, his ears laid flat back. Jonathan laughed. Ruth was still sitting on Bright Morning and had not foreseen, until it happened, the next move.

Mrs. Meredith, still holding Toad, turned to Peter on Sirius and said, 'You take Toad, Peter, and Jonathan can try Sirius.'

Peter got off and gave his reins to Jonathan, and came over to

Toad. Ruth was watching him closely, so angry that she could feel herself shaking. She could tell that it was exactly what Peter wanted, and yet not to show her anything; it was for himself. He took Toad's reins, and ran a hand down his neck just behind his ear and said something to him, then he mounted and lengthened the stirrups, and rode away towards the jumps. Toad went quietly, but very alert, all collected up but not pulling. He looked beautiful, Ruth thought painfully, everything a ridden animal should be. She had never felt so wounded. He broke into a perfect collected canter, and jumped flawlessly, and then cantered on calmly in a large circle back to his place in the line. Peter did not look at Ruth. Ruth felt as if her whole head was full of tears, crowding to burst out. She stared at her hands, clamped on Bright Morning's snaffle rein, not daring to move or look at anybody. Then, at her side, Jonathan said softly, 'You're not the only one with troubles.'

He was on Sirius, looking worried. Ruth recognized the sympathy that had prompted his words, but felt worse rather than better. It was a minute or two before she dared lift her eyes and by then there was plenty of distraction, for Sirius was playing up in front of the cavalettis. Having successfully stopped him from tearing off, Jonathan was now having difficulty in making him go forward, the pony napping and running backwards. Mrs. Meredith said to Peter, 'I don't want to undo any of your work on that pony. Would you rather Jonathan didn't ride him? Do you want to take him again?'

'What he's doing now, he would do with me as well,' Peter said. 'It's not Jonathan.'

'This is quite normal?'

'Yes. He doesn't like waiting around.'

Mrs. Meredith looked gloomy, and glanced at her watch. Down the field, the others had finished and were going back to the stables.

'Do you think you're going to cure him of all his traumas by the summer?' Mrs. Meredith asked Peter. 'Are you sure you're not wasting your time?'

'I might be,' Peter said. Ruth recognized his polite, contained expression. He was hating Mrs. Meredith. She realized in that moment, the truth of Jonathan's remark: 'You're not the only one with troubles.' Mr. McNair had said Sirius needed a bullet. No doubt he had told Mrs. Meredith the same. Peter was as stubborn as she was, when it came to choosing an unsuitable animal. The only difference was, he knew what he was doing, and she didn't. She felt a small bond reach out towards Peter, even though he was still sitting on Toad. She was forced into an unnatural role, hating him, when really they had everything in common, including all the faults—taking it all too seriously and not heeding the advice of their elders and betters. The whole thing was ridiculous, that it mattered, but she could tell by Peter's face that it mattered terribly that he was going to work it out with Sirius, just as it mattered to her with Toad. They were both stupid.

'It's good for Jonathan,' Mrs. Meredith said, watching thoughtfully. 'He's not used to this sort of thing.'

'He made Railway,' Peter said, almost belligerent.

Mrs. Meredith gave him a slightly surprised look, and said crisply, 'Railway was perfectly straightforward. A strange character, but no vices.' She was implying that Sirius's misbehaviour came into the vice category.

Peter said no more. Ruth, knowing him so well, knew that he was having to be very careful not to be rude. He got off Toad, watching Sirius all the time. Jonathan called out to him, 'Do you want him? I'm not getting anywhere.'

Peter went out and they changed places, and Peter started to walk Sirius round in circles, away from the jumps.

'The rest of us might as well call it a day,' Mrs. Meredith said.

They got back on to their own ponies, and started towards the gate. Mrs. Meredith walked beside Ruth, and said, 'You've got a difficult task there, Ruth. You will have to be very patient, lots of calm work in the school, and very small jumps, slowly. It will take time. He's a splendid pony.'

'For Peter.'

'Nothing comes easily, Ruth. We all have our teething troubles. And Peter has a harder job than you, I think.'

Mr. McNair was waiting in the yard, having driven back to collect Peter. Mrs. Meredith told him what had happened and Mr. McNair swore and said, 'He'll be all afternoon, if I know that pair. I rue the day I set eyes on that pony, Mrs. Meredith. Life's too short for coping with that sort of animal these days.'

'Well, Peter will do it if anyone will.'

Jonathan said good-bye to Ruth and Thea and went to put

Railway away. Mr. McNair went grumbling down the field to hurry Peter up. Mrs. Meredith went across to Railway's loose box and said to Jonathan, 'You'll have to be quick. The dentist's appointment is at two and I want to call at Hatchett's on the way there.'

'You shouldn't have asked Peter to ride Toad,' Jonathan said. 'It wasn't fair.'

Mrs. Meredith looked at Jonathan, frowning. 'I didn't—' she started tartly, then paused. Her tone changed. 'I put Ruth on Bright Morning to restore her confidence, which worked. Then the temptation was too much for me. I wanted to see how much difference there would be in Toad, with Peter.'

'Yes, well, Ruth saw it too. She's not dim, you know. I think it was cruel.'

'Perhaps. But it might have worked the other way. I wasn't sure if this Peter and Toad combination wasn't a myth.'

'It wasn't a myth. It was true.'

'Yes. I'm afraid it was. If only we could have Peter on Toad for our team! Oh dear, what potential there, and Peter going to waste on that devil of an animal!'

'It's the people that matter,' Jonathan said. 'A team is the people.'

His voice was low and his mother didn't hear. Scowling dreadfully, Jonathan pulled off his hat and loosened the knot of his tie, and scuffled his way towards the house.

Out in the field, Peter was jumping Sirius over the cavalettis, slowly and with great precision.

9

THEA said to Ruth, 'You *must* enter. It's only a potty little show, in aid of somebody's Village Hall, and the opposition will be absolutely nil. It's exactly the sort of show to enter Toad for the first time. Nothing to be frightened of at all.'

'Well, I suppose I've got to start some time,' Ruth said. 'You don't think Mrs. Meredith is likely to be there?'

'No. Impossible. It's the same day as the Drayton Point-to-Point. Absolutely no one will be there.'

Ruth remembered these words when she arrived at the show-

ground with Thea, and saw a beautifully laid out ring with proper
B.S.J.A. jumps and rows of horse-boxes lined up under the trees.
It was a warm spring day and everybody was there. Not the
Merediths, true, but Peter McNair was in the Secretary's tent
collecting his number for Sirius for the 14.2 class.

Ruth glared at Thea and backed out abruptly, pushing her way
past the queue. Thea followed her. Ruth knew she had to go through
with it, without Thea telling her, but she felt she had to organize
her wits before she actually committed herself and collected her
number.

'You are an idiot!' Thea said, not unkindly.

'I'll wait till Peter's gone,' Ruth said.

'It doesn't *matter*,' Thea said. 'You don't have to care so much.
Toad will be all right. You've just got to steer him properly, that's
all. You know you can do it.'

'Yes,' Ruth said.

She was improving, it was true, but so brash to try in public
already . . . 'You said it was going to be a potty little show! Look
at it—'

'There's only Peter who's anyone, and he's only here because
it's a potty little show as well. He's more reason to feel worried
than you.'

'I wish I hadn't come.'

'No, well, you have come, and you'll be glad afterwards,' Thea
said, perhaps with more conviction than she felt. 'It's a lovely big
ring—no tricks. Perfect for first time.'

Ruth was glad that Thea was there to force her. She went back
into the tent and collected her number. The Secretary was a
motherly soul, obviously a Village Hall woman, at sea with
horses.

'Are you sure we've got his name right? Toadhill Flax? Isn't
it rather odd?'

'No, that's right.'

'Number eighteen, class seven.'

'Thank you.'

Thea was seventeen and Peter was twenty-one. There was
plenty of time, the 13.2 hand class having only just started. The
standard was encouragingly low, many of the ponies refusing at
the first fence and getting eliminated. Ruth and Thea stood watching, Thea laughing, Ruth preoccupied. A narrow-faced little girl

in a black jacket, blonde hair tied back with large red ribbons, rode into the ring and gave her pony a determined belt before it had even seen the first jump. It bounded off, head in the air, and the girl wrenched it back, using some unchildlike language. Ruth came out of her dream with a start.

'It's Fly!'

The sight was painful in the extreme. It would have been painful whatever the pony, but to see her own Fly-by-Night the victim of such bad riding took Ruth's mind abruptly off all her other troubles. Fly had been an eager jumper when she sold him, but his new rider had obviously given him a distaste for the job, probably because of the way she hung on to his mouth all the time. He approached the first jump sideways, hanging back, and the girl gave him a series of enormous thumps in the belly with her heels, and two or three lashes of her crop for good measure. Fly spun round and presented his tail to the jump, ready to buck, and the girl hauled him round to face it again and swore at him, thumping and beating. It was impossible for Fly to jump, even had he wished to, without room to take off and with his mouth held tightly by angry hands, so he stood there with his ears laid back, sidling and snorting, until he knocked the jump over with his forelegs, then he scrambled over the mess and trotted miserably on towards the next one, head down and hocks trailing. The girl hit him again and he bucked and she went over his head. She landed on her feet, practised at falling off, and pulled Fly's head round sharply and attempted to mount. But Fly wisely kept going round in circles until a steward came to hold him, then, when she was aboard again, he would only go backwards, until the bell sounded for elimination.

Ruth watched this sorry performance with horror. She saw the girl ride Fly furiously out of the ring, beating him with her crop, and heard a woman next to her click her tongue and say, 'What a nasty sight! Show-jumping does have its unpleasant side, I'm afraid.'

Ruth thrust Toad's reins into Thea's hands and hurried off in pursuit of Fly. She was so angry and distressed that she acted instinctively, without thinking. She ran after the girl and caught her up just as she reached her parents' car. The familiar father in the trendy boots was standing there looking furious.

'He's no good! He's useless!' the child shouted at her father, adding several sanguinary epithets to relieve her feelings. Her small, white face was screwed up with humiliation.

'It's you!' Ruth darted at her furiously. 'How do you expect him to do anything when you ride him like that? How can he jump with you heaving at his mouth all the time? It's not *him*! You aren't fit to have a pony, the way you ride!'

'Just a minute, my girl, who do you think you're talking to?' The father turned on her, coldly angry.

Ruth was in no state to temper her opinion. 'You've no right to have a pony, treating him like that! You—'

'Hang on, hang on! Who do you think you are, telling us what to do?'

'You know who I am,' Ruth said rashly. 'I sold you the pony, and if I'd known what a rotten rider your daughter was I would never have—'

'Yes, my girl, and if I'd known what a rotten pony I was buying I'd never have gone through with the deal! I like your cheek, young woman! Just you keep a check on your tongue, or I'll fetch the police to you.'

Ruth, her eyes on Fly's miserable condition, said hotly: 'You call the police—I'd be pleased! You could be reported for the way you treated Fly, all that beating! And just look at him—why, his mouth is bleeding, the way you pull him about—' She was beside herself, examining Fly closely, seeing hairless spur marks on his sides, his summer coat staring and dull, his jaunty demeanour turned sour. Quite a few people had gathered round to listen to the exchange, grinning.

'You run along now,' the man said crisply. 'Or I'll come round and have a word with your father.'

'Are you having trouble?' Ruth felt a hand drop on her shoulder and found Ted standing beside her. He was addressing his words to Fly's owner, not to Ruth. 'I'll remove her, if you like.'

'I'll be glad to see the back of her, yes. Just cut along and keep your nose out of other people's business.'

'But it is my business!' Ruth raged. 'Can't you see—'

Ted put his hand firmly round the back of her neck and steered her away in the opposite direction. Brute force propelled her through the grinning throng.

'For Heaven's sake, you young maniac, you can't go round insulting people like that! Have you gone potty?'

'Did you see—did you see what she did—how she rode Fly?'
Ruth choked, the tears spilling up. 'He looked awful! I must—I
must do something—I—'

'Ruth, stop it! Pull yourself together! You need a flaming
keeper, the way you carry on. Not fit to be let out on your own.
You've come here expressly to have a fun day. Now get on with it.
Here.' He handed her a large oily handkerchief. 'Mum and Dad
have come, all smiling and happy, to cheer you on, and here you
are, running amok in the crowd. You'd have had a copper there
any minute. Thea told me—'

'Did you see poor Fly? How she beat him? We must buy him
back—honestly, we must! We can't let him—'

'Ruth! Shut up! There's no money to buy him back with. I've
spent it. So shut up.'

'I can sell Toad—'

'Oh, you're demented! Out of your mind. The man doesn't
want to sell Fly. And you certainly don't want him back, having
gone to such maniacal lengths to replace him with money you
never had in the first place. Stop blathering and grow up.'

He looked angry. Ruth blew her nose loudly into his handkerchief and tried to pull herself together.

'You look awful,' Ted said. 'Calm down. I'll buy you an ice-
cream to cool off.'

'I don't want one. What shall I do?'

'Absolutely nothing. Just shut up and think about something
else.'

'How can I?'

'Grow up!'

Ruth tried to do all the things Ted advised, but she could not
calm the raging indignation inside her. It was strongly laced with
guilt and remorse, and kept coming up into her throat as if it
would choke her. She walked about with Ted, not noticing anything, or being able to think of anything else at all, until suddenly
Thea appeared before her, looking hot and anxious and said, 'For
goodness' sake! I've been looking for you all over the place! I'm
in next, and then it's you.'

Ruth nearly panicked. Ted took her firmly by the arm and
steered her towards the collecting ring, where her mother was
holding Toad and looking worried.

'Whatever have you been doing? We thought you'd got lost!'

'Oh, my number—! I've lost it—I—'

'In your pocket,' Ted said.

He tied it on her, while she heaved up Toad's girths. She didn't feel that anything was quite real. No time even to get frightened. She mounted just as Thea came out of the ring. She had had no time to see what Thea had done, but Thea pulled up in a flurry beside her and said, 'One knock-down! Don't forget to wait for the starting bell. Good luck!'

'Number eighteen?' The steward was ticking off his list.

'Yes.'

'Off you go.'

The ring was there before her, all her own. Toad started to yo-yo. Ruth remembered the drill and steered him for the judge's caravan at the side of the ring, to show her number. She intended to trot, but Toad insisted on cantering. She tore past the judges, but managed to pull up and come round towards the start moderately under control. The bell pinged. Toad plunged towards the first fence. No time now to consider anything but the job in hand. Suddenly it seemed to her that anything was possible: with the first jump looming up, and knowing that Toad could do it, there weren't any problems. He was going fast, but perfectly on course, and not out of hand. Ruth looked steadfastly between his eagerly pricked ears at the unassuming brush fence, and they were over it before she had time to doubt. It felt wonderful, and Ruth saw no reason at all why it shouldn't continue that way. She felt very clear-headed, and full of confidence. Toad was pulling, but not with malice or frustration, merely with an inclination to get on with the job, and Ruth felt as eager. There was no time to analyse this extraordinary recipe for certain success: the jumps came up fast, Ruth faced Toad at them, steadied him as best she could and hoped desperately for the best. If the ring had been smaller and the jumps closer together, Toad would probably have knocked them flying or run out, but the space was so generous that there was room to turn without overshooting, even with what Ruth thought of as her inadequate riding, her feeble legs and insecure seat.

By the time she was three-quarters of the way round without a fault, she had gained such confidence that she actually felt capable of placing Toad at the jump just where she wanted him. Whether it was a mere illusion of grandeur or the real thing she never knew, but he jumped the final wall and the triple-bar with impeccable

79

judgement, beautifully balanced, and left the ring at a contained trot to a warm round of applause. Ruth was speechless with astonishment.

Thea and Ted and her mother and father came to meet her looking equally astonished and delighted.

'I knew you could!' Thea shouted, beaming. 'It was a marvellous round!'

'Splendid, Ruth!' said her father, looking proud and amazed. 'I didn't know you'd got him going so well!'

Nor did Ruth. 'I can't believe it!' It was all she could say. It was so totally unexpected; she had been utterly unprepared, no time to be frightened. Her mind had actually been on something else altogether.

She looked round at everything very carefully, to make quite sure that she wasn't dreaming and—to convince her—she saw Peter entering the ring on Sirius. As usual, he wasn't giving anything away; he looked very serious, concentrating hard. He must have seen her moment of triumph. She imagined it must have been as much a shock to him as it had been to her and no doubt he intended to beat her. Knowing the way he felt, she knew that in fact he was utterly determined to beat her.

'He'll be lucky to get a clear round,' Thea said.

'How many did?'

'You were the fourth.'

'So there'll be a jump-off.'

'Yes.'

Ruth watched Peter closely, praying that Sirius would hit something. It wasn't that she wanted to win, but she didn't want a confrontation with Peter. She didn't want all this Peter-thing to get tangled up with what at the moment was her plain and glorious break-through with Toad. Sirius was looking wild, eager to jump, and not nappy. Peter's main problem was exactly the same as hers, to control him sufficiently for accurate jumping.

'I'd rather have Toad any day,' Thea said feelingly, watching.

'So would Peter.'

'Toad might be difficult, but at least he's safe.'

'Poor Peter.' Ruth felt a great rush of genuine sympathy for his problems, having momentarily no cause for self-pity. Sirius was jumping magnificently but was very hard to hold. Peter had him in a fairly hefty bit, but was allowing him as much freedom as he dared, and was coming in to his jumps very fast. It was a spectacular round, and more spectacular as it progressed, Sirius gaining confidence in his freedom and jumping with hair-raising generosity. Ruth, watching, felt herself shrinking inside. The last thing she desired was a jump-off with Peter.

Sirius came round the last corner to head down the centre towards the wall and the triple-bar. He overshot, as Toad had done, and Peter had to do a U-turn and then swing round on the other leg. Sirius, pulling like mad, half-reared several times as Peter attempted to steady him, then plunged off at full speed. Peter did not try to hold him back. Sirius flew the wall with about two feet to spare, and bore down on the triple without a pause. Peter was forced to take a pull at him this time, but Sirius responded nobly, gathered himself together and took off exactly right for another magnificent jump.

Ruth felt her stomach turn over miserably.

'Fantastic!' Thea said.

Peter came out of the ring, soothing Sirius, who was covered in sweat. Close to, he looked very wild and upset and, to Ruth, horrifyingly powerful. Everyone shrank back and rode their horses tactfully and rapidly out of the way, and Peter brought Sirius to a trembling halt. He sat stroking his neck, relaxing the reins. Sirius snatched at the bit, stretching out his head, but then seemed content. Peter looked pleased. He saw Thea and Ruth and nodded at them happily.

'Marvellous round!' Thea said. 'Well done!'

Ruth could not bring herself to say anything.

The steward came over to her and said, 'Number eighteen? You'll be riding again. Don't go away.'

'Oh heavens.' Ruth felt numb. 'Thea, do you think—'

'Toad is going marvellously,' Thea said urgently. 'Much better than Sirius. You've nothing to worry about. Don't be so *stupid*!'

Ruth decided she hadn't got a competitive temperament. She went all to pieces. It must go through to Toad, her great shaking lack of confidence. But this time—this time was going to be different. She kept well clear of Peter, who was walking Sirius about to calm him down.

The steward said, 'It'll be just the first three jumps and the last two. Not against the clock—we haven't got a timing apparatus.'

They drew for order, and Peter had to go first.

He went out into the ring, sideways, Sirius lifting his feet up very high. He went crabwise all the way to the first jump, cantering like a rocking-horse. Peter swung him into it almost at the last stride, giving him plenty of rein, and Sirius took off with his usual frantic bound and flew over. Peter, perhaps feeling that the pony was likely to get out of control, obviously did not intend to give him so much freedom in this round, but Sirius resisted bitterly, and fought against the bit, tearing at Peter's hands. Ruth and Thea watched anxiously.

'He's crazy to ride that pony,' Thea said.

'I think he just wants to see what'll he do in public,' Ruth said. 'He seems to have got him settled down at home.'

'Yes, well, oh God Almighty! Look at him.'

It was hypnotic to watch, with what looked like certain disaster close at hand, but Peter's determination was a match for Sirius. Unable to tear away, he half-reared towards the jumps, leaping forward off his hind legs like something in a circus, and each time Peter let him go a few strides before the jump, so that he positively exploded over the obstacle, jumping so easily and freely that he made four feet look more like four inches. He knocked nothing down, and the loud-speaker announced a clear round.

'That's the winner,' Ruth said.

82

'Idiot!' Thea said. 'Poor Toad, having you! Get on now. He's dying to sail round again!'

It *must* be easy for her, Ruth thought, compared to Peter's task. She sent Toad into the ring, praying hard. He went straight into a fast canter towards the first jump, but she had to circle first as the bell hadn't gone, and Toad was annoyed and gave a small buck. She sat back a bit and steadied him, pulling fairly hard, then the bell went and she could head him in the right direction. She felt as keen as he did, and they flew it in famous style. On to the next: the feel of it, powerful and willing, went to her head, and she felt as confidently the winner now as she had felt about Peter a few moments earlier. The jumps were in one big circle, and she came to the third, two red and white poles, rather more powerfully and willingly than was wise, and it was more by Toad's cleverness than her own that they survived. He stood too far back and had to make a great reaching jump to clear it. Ruth listened tensely for the familiar sound of bouncing poles, but there was nothing but the thudding of Toad's eager hooves bearing down dangerously fast towards the wall. She tried to pull him up a bit, but was frightened to interfere too much. Better to sit, and hope for the best, and try and pull up a bit afterwards, ready for the triple. Toad knew more about it than she did. His long white mane flew back in her face. She saw the red face of the wall, and felt him reach out beneath her, very sure and strong. It was all right; he trusted her now, and they were both game for the triple-bars. They were jumping much too fast, but Toad cleared the bars with as much to spare as Sirius, and pulled up without any trouble, snorting with great cart-horse snorts of satisfaction. Ruth rode back into the collecting ring feeling that she was ready for anything: Hickstead, Wembley . . . they would be nothing to them.

Peter was sitting there on Sirius, watching her. She felt herself going crimson. She didn't want it spoiled by any ill feeling. But it was impossible to say anything to Peter, the way he was looking. Very frosty and far-away. Thea rode over, smiling with excitement.

'Oh, lovely! He was wonderful! Well done!'

Peter turned Sirius away. Ruth could feel her self-satisfaction bursting out, swelling her up, a great bolster of marvellous content, not like poker-faced Peter, who had done it all a thousand times before. She tried to contain herself, to look as if it was nothing, but she could not get the great stupid grin off her face. Thea was laughing. There were two more ponies to go. They sat and watched.

Thea said, 'Peter's father doesn't know he's here, did you know? He hacked over. His father said he wasn't to enter.'

Ruth was impressed, knowing how nasty father McNair could be when disobeyed.

'Father McNair apparently thinks Sirius isn't worth spending time on, and Peter wants to prove he is.'

'Well, he's proved it all right so far.' The competitor they were watching obligingly knocked down the gate, and Ruth tried to look sympathetic, but couldn't. She had a nasty feeling that Peter and she might have to jump off again. She didn't want to.

'He's third, at least,' Thea said. The fourth competitor knocked the gate down as well, and two bricks out of the wall.

'Second, at least,' Thea amended. 'First or second.'

'We haven't got to go again?' Ruth was appalled. She had never planned a confrontation with Peter; it was extraordinary the way it had worked out, as if Fate was having a bit of fun at their expense. She didn't think Peter wanted it very much either. The steward, having conferred with the judges, came over busily.

'Twenty-one!' he bawled at Peter. 'Eighteen and twenty-one!'

Peter rode over, looking stony.

'Do you want to share the first or jump-off again?' the steward asked. 'The judges don't mind either way. Last two jumps only, if you decide to jump-off.'

'Share,' Ruth said.

'Jump-off,' Peter said.

The steward looked at them both in turn, waiting for an amicable agreement, but nothing happened. He said to Peter, 'You're sure you won't share?'

'No, I won't,' Peter said. 'If she won't jump off, I'll take first.'

'Oh no, you won't,' Ruth said.

'You'll jump off then?' the steward asked.

'Yes,' Ruth said.

'I'll tell the judges.'

He hurried away again and two more stewards put another row of bricks on the wall, and notched the triple up one hole. Ruth watched gloomily. She hadn't wanted this at all. She wanted to win but she didn't want to beat Peter. She didn't want him to beat her either. She wanted to share the prize, and for Peter to be pleased because he had done superbly well with Sirius, and to be friends again. She looked at him, prepared to say all this, but his expression was grim. She supposed, if it was true what Thea said about his father having forbidden him to come, that it would be far more convincing, with the big row looming on the horizon, to have a red rosette to flourish in justification rather than a blue one. To her, the old friendship was more important than anything, but boys, of course, were apt to be incomprehensible and piggish. It didn't seem that there was anything she could do to cure the present situation.

The steward came back with a penny to toss for the order of jumping. Peter called and lost, so had to go first. He shortened his reins and took Sirius into the ring, and Sirius, seeing the green grass and the coloured jumps yet again, gathered himself together, straining to go, raking out against Peter's restraint, flecks of white lather flying from the bit. He was a spectacularly powerful pony, not a miniature thoroughbred, but more a scaled-down hunter, compact and deep-through, but with a fine head and neck that gave him his classy, flashy look, and it was impossible not to admire the picture he made, tearing towards the wall, however undesirable it in fact was. Ruth was holding her breath. It did look terribly fast. Remembering the bolting performance she had witnessed a little earlier in the year, she was slightly apprehensive. It all put Toad's impetuosity in a much better light, by comparison: Toad was merely eager. Sirius looked bent on destruction.

He jumped so big over the wall that Peter slightly lost balance. It was exactly as it had happened before. Letting the reins run out so as not to interfere with the pony's head, Peter was not in time to gather them together to check Sirius when he was most receptive to being checked, away from the jump. With any other pony it wouldn't have mattered, but this time Sirius was away, not merely fast, but dangerously fast. The ring was large, but it was surrounded thickly by goggling spectators, cars and horses, and it was no place to be bolted with. Peter sat back and heaved, not bothered about jumping the triple-bar so much as getting back in control. Whatever it was that happened, happened so fast that Ruth was never quite sure exactly what it was. Thea said it was the wet grass, and that Sirius, checked so strongly, slipped, but Ruth was only aware of a sudden flurry of horse and rider apparently turning a somersault right into the wings of the triple-bar, which disintegrated, the poles scattering. There was an awful noise of splintering wood.

85

Sirius was down and Peter appeared to be underneath him in a tangle of reins and poles. The stewards started running.

'Ugh!' Ruth felt sick. She saw Sirius scramble to his feet and look around, then start trotting away, but Peter didn't move.

'Oh, God!' Ruth said. 'He's killed himself.'

'He'll be all right,' Thea said.

Ruth knew riders usually bounced. But the little knot of people gathered round Peter didn't seem to be getting him on his feet at all. The ambulance men ran out, hopefully carrying a stretcher. Ruth, remembering that Peter had come to the show alone, said, 'We'd better get Sirius. There's no one else.' Some one had caught him but looked very nervous. Ruth got off Toad, threw his reins to Thea, and ran out into the ring. She took Sirius off the relieved man, and sorted out his trailing reins and stroked his neck. Having come to a standstill, he was very jumpy, but did not seem disposed to go tearing off any more. Ruth turned him round and approached the group round Peter. The ambulance men had taken charge and Peter was laid out on his back. He appeared to be struggling to get up, and was being restrained, as Ruth could hear him saying something, but it did sound rather unlike his usual laconic tones, almost hysterical. His face was covered with blood and his white shirt was spattered with red in a most lavish, televisual fashion, clashing horribly with his purple Pony Club tie. Ruth stared, aghast. He appeared to be saying something to her, but the ambulance men kept interfering with bland reassurance as if to a three-year-old: 'Take it easy, laddie. Steady on now.'

'Sirius,' he said. 'Don't let Dad—'

'Just take it easy now. Don't worry about anything. Everything's all right.'

'Ruth—don't let him—'

Ruth got up close, stepping over one of the ambulance men. 'I won't let him,' she said loudly and clearly. 'I'll look after him, I promise—'

'Just move back, miss, if you please!' The voice was sharp.

They lifted Peter on to the stretcher. He gave an awful moan and lay back suddenly very quiet and still, while the ambulance man was still saying, 'That's it, laddie. There's nothing to worry about.'

'There bloody well is,' Ruth stormed. There was everything in the world. Peter had lapsed into unconsciousness, steeped in the most awful problems, and would have them with him as large as life

86

when he woke up again. If he ever did. The tears poured down
Ruth's cheeks. Her mother was there suddenly, walking beside the
stretcher. She said, 'I'll go to hospital with him, and stay with him
until somebody comes. With luck I'll be back to see to the supper.
I'll ring the McNairs from the hospital.'

'They don't know,' Ruth said. 'That he's here. His father forbad
him to come.'

'Oh, you children!' Her mother rolled her eyes. 'I can see why.'

'Don't let Mr. McNair—'

'No, I won't. Don't be silly.'

Ruth went back to the collecting ring with Sirius and went up to
Thea. Before she could say anything the steward came up and said,
'Number eighteen, hurry up now! It's your turn. Are you ready?'

'What for?'

He stared at her. Ruth came to with a start. 'Oh, golly, but—'
But what?

'Go *on*', Thea said.

Ruth gave her Sirius's reins and got back on to Toad. She rode
into the ring and cantered fast down to the far end. She could only
think of Peter disappearing in all that mess of scrabbling hooves
and flying timber. She didn't feel that anything else was very real
at all. It felt very strange to be on Toad, bearing down on the large,
blood-red wall. This was just what Peter had been doing a few
minutes before. It wasn't really very difficult at all. They were over
it and bearing down on the triple-bars. Ruth remembered thinking
that it couldn't possibly happen twice. The bars loomed up. Toad
gave a little lurch, jumped, and hit the top bar. It came down with
a resonant crash behind them, but Toad cantered on happily. Ruth
pulled up and walked back to the collecting ring.

'He slipped in the same place,' Thea said. 'That's why you hit
it. But you've won, all the same.'

She should have felt very happy, but couldn't.

Even Thea was cast down, in spite of being tough and hard.
'Was Peter all right? He didn't look it very.'

'No. He looked awful. He passed out. But he was all het up
about Sirius. He said 'Don't let Dad—' and stopped. I imagine he
meant shoot him. I said I wouldn't.'

'God! It's the best thing. He's awful. Dangerous, I mean.'

'What, to be shot?'

'Yes. Even hacking, he's a bolter.'

'You couldn't.'

Ruth looked at him, the beautiful pony, standing nervously at their side, his coat dark with sweat.

'It's not his fault,' she said vehemently. 'How can you say that? You can't shoot him, because he's only what people have *made* him. You should shoot the people who made him like that.'

'I think you ought to take her home,' Ted said to Thea. 'Before someone shuts her away.'

'She's got to go and get her rosette,' Thea said. 'Go on, you idiot. They're shouting for you.'

Ruth rode into the ring, still incensed. She felt very close to Peter, desperate to get his message out before he was carted away. He felt the same as she did, she knew. If she was potty, he was too. But nobody else seemed to share their particular brand of mental aberration. She took her red rosette, and the blue one for Peter, without any sense of accomplishment, her mind entirely occupied with the new events that had just been thrown at her. She did her circuit of the ring with the other winners, and rode back to Thea immediately.

'I suppose we've got to take Sirius back,' Thea said. 'There's no one else to take him.'

'I'm going to take him home with me,' Ruth said. 'I promised Peter. To look after him I mean.'

'You can't stop McNair shooting him if he wants to. It's his pony, and he's only protecting Peter, after all.'

'Well, I've got to stave him off until Peter is well enough to argue himself. I promised him.'

'Rather you than me. I'm going to enter for the Scurry.'

'There's the Open to come first. And the Novice. It'll be ages.'

'Yes. I don't mind. It's all right for you—you've got your rosette.'

'Yes! Fantastic! I think I'll go home then, because of Sirius.'

Toad was too small for the Open and not eligible for the Novice, and her mind was all over the place.

'Can you manage with the two of them?'

'I think so.'

Sirius seemed quiet enough, positively subdued, after the afternoon's capers. Thea handed over the reins, and Ruth started for home. She had so much on her mind that she never thought to worry about any possible difficulties. Her fantastic success with

Toad kept bubbling up through all the dark thoughts. She had Toad beneath her, friendly and familiar, his cocky red ears pricked up and his white mane blowing out in the breeze, and the lovely Sirius at her side, stepping out with his neck arched, his stride very long and easy. She could well see what Peter liked about him. She sensed that there was, in fact, something of Toad about him, although it was hard to say exactly why. When she put him in the loose box, she stood talking to him for a bit; he was uneasy and stood very still and tense, listening. She looked into his black, nervous eyes, and wondered what was inside his brain. Was he thinking, did he remember? Did horses know anything, beyond what they saw, what they remembered? Did he really equate jumps with fear, because he had been beaten over them, or was he just a stupid, senseless brute, reacting without reason? She could not accept this last possibility. She wanted passionately to protect him from the fate Mr. McNair was wishing on him. She had promised anyway. She had no option.

Her mother came home fairly soon afterwards.

'There was no point staying,' she said. 'He's out cold, and they don't think he'll come round for some time. He's got concussion and he's badly bruised and got some nasty cuts, but nothing else as far as they can tell at the moment. So it could be worse, I suppose. Poor Peter. Nothing broken.'

'Did you see his father?'

'No. I rang him. You were right about him not knowing Peter had gone to that show. He sounded furious—that's why I didn't wait. I didn't want to get too involved. I don't care for him when he's in that mood. Oh dear, the scrapes you children get into! I can't think why Peter wanted to do it, knowing what his father thought about the whole business—'

'Well, if he'd won, he'd have shown his father that Sirius is worth keeping.'

'He's proved exactly the opposite, I would have thought.'

'Yes, well, it went wrong.'

Ruth wondered if McNair was going to sit by Peter's bedside waiting for him to come round. What a nasty awakening for Peter. At any rate, while Sirius was safe in her loose box, Peter need have nothing to fear.

Two hours later there was a knock at the door and Mr. McNair was standing on the doorstep.

'Oh, hullo, come in,' Ruth said trying to look polite.

He came in. 'Have you got my horse ?'

'Yes.'

'Oh, thank God for that. I've been chasing around trying to find out what had happened to it half the night. None of the show organizers had any idea. And I want to see your mother and thank her for what she did.'

Ruth took him into the living-room to her mother and father who looked slightly apprehensive.

'How is Peter ?'

'He was coming to when I left him. The doctor thought it wasn't worth my staying, so I didn't. I'd only have been angry, which wouldn't have helped. Wait till he's fully conscious though—' he broke off, shrugging. 'That boy, he's as perverse as they come. The hours of good time he's wasted on that animal! I told him after the first hour it was too far gone to bother with. I don't mind if they're just green, or got into a few bad habits, but I draw the line at dangerous animals. Especially ponies. I'll never sell that one on. More than my job's worth. There's only one thing for that fellow. I'll go back and get the trailer, if that's convenient by you, and take him back with me. It was very kind of you, Ruth, to bring him down here.'

'I don't mind keeping him a bit,' Ruth said. 'Don't bother about fetching him, really. It's nice for Toad to have company.'

'He's no bother ?'

'No, honestly.'

'Well, in that case, I can give Roberts a ring in the morning and he can collect him himself. Save me the trouble.'

Roberts was the local slaughterer.

'No!' Ruth said. 'You can't do that!'

Mr. McNair looked at her, surprised. Ruth struggled, remembering that she was considered barmy. With a great effort she said, very collectedly, 'I think you should leave him here just a day or two until Peter is quite better. Concussion is brain damage, and if Peter finds out what's happened it might affect him. I'm sure the doctor would think that.'

They all looked at her as if what she said was well worth considering. To her infinite relief, her mother said, 'Yes, it could upset Peter very badly, in his present condition. I'm sure there's no hurry on our part for you to take him away.'

'No, truly, our grass needs eating down,' Ruth said. 'It would do us a favour. Toad is getting much too fat on it.'

'Hmm.' McNair frowned. 'Perhaps we'd better get Peter straight. I don't want him going funny on me again—any more of this psychiatrist lark. We can always turn the brute out until Peter's forgotten about him, I suppose. Peter is very fond of him, it's true. Like Toad all over again, and I regretted getting rid of *him*, the way things turned out. You could be right. He certainly won't be riding him any more, though.' He turned to go, declining a cup of coffee. 'I've troubled you enough for one day, one way or another. I'm very grateful to you for all you've done. Very kind.'

He took his leave, and Mrs. Hollis closed the door thoughtfully behind him.

'Poor Peter,' she said. 'No wonder he has to turn to horses for a bit of affection. Quite bright of you, Ruth, stalling him like that.'

Ted looked up from the television set, which he had been watching all the time. 'You see?' he said to Ruth. 'The adult approach works. Not like the other little performance you put on this afternoon. Peter will give you his undying gratitude for saving his naggie's life.'

Ted had noticed the great effort she had made. She might have guessed. Fly-by-Night—oh God! That was another problem in her in-tray . . .

IO

PETER'S undying gratitude was not at all apparent when Ruth visited him in hospital with Thea two days later. She hadn't wanted to go, but Thea persuaded her, saying that it was their duty, and when she got there, face to face, she knew that her instincts had been right, as they unfailingly were. Peter gave her a very ungracious look, and spoke to Thea. Ruth sat on the end of the bed. It was the accident ward, where Ted had been for three months after falling off his motor bike; she felt quite at home. Peter was lying down, and said he wasn't allowed to sit up. He showed them some very impressive bruises on his right arm and shoulder. There was a bad cut on his cheek, and he looked yellowish, but otherwise all right.

'I've brought your rosette,' Ruth said, and knew that it wasn't tactful. He took it and threw it on his locker, but it fell on the floor. Thea was grovelling for it when Mrs. Meredith arrived, looking as efficient and purposeful as usual. Ruth saw Peter make an effort to pull himself together and felt a pang of sympathy. Mrs. Meredith was formidable enough when one was in the full flower of health; her visit would probably set Peter's recovery back by one or two days.

'Hullo, all of you. I'm sorry to hear about this, Peter. Not like you at all. I thought you always bounced. Fall on you, did he? The ground's hard too, no give at all.'

'He slipped,' Peter said. He didn't say that he had been bolting at the time.

'I hear your father's not too pleased?'

'Not overjoyed, no,' Peter said.

'And how long are you going to be laid off for? We want you riding again as soon as possible—you're no good to us like this.'

'I don't know. They won't say.'

'Sirius not hurt?'

Peter hesitated.

'No,' Ruth said. 'He's fine.' Not dead yet, she thought. 'He's at my place,' she added. 'I'm looking after him.'

'Father wants him shot,' Peter said. 'But I told him if he did I—' He paused. 'Well—'

'What would you do?' Mrs. Meredith looked at him sharply.

'Leave home.'

'It wouldn't do you any good,' Mrs. Meredith said severely. 'I don't know what gets into you young people today, that you reject so utterly what is done for you—offered to you—entirely in your own interests.'

There was a rather pointed silence. Peter stared at the ceiling and Thea picked at the label on the lemonade bottle on the locker.

Ruth guessed that Mrs. Meredith was thinking of Jonathan, as well as Peter.

'Did Florestan do well on Saturday?' Ruth asked her, very politely.

'Third. Not bad, considering the opposition. There was a young horse in the Maiden Race, a brown gelding, very nice. Your father has his eye on him, I think, Peter.'

'Solomon's Seal.'

'That's the one. I think he's gone over to see the owners today.

93

He told me that he would like to see you on a bigger animal—a young one you can start eventing on.'

'Hmm.' Peter went on staring at the ceiling.

'If you've got a father who'll think of buying you a horse like that, you're not so badly off, Peter.' Mrs. Meredith smiled kindly.

Peter did not reply. He could be beautifully rude without being embarrassed. Ruth envied him the gift.

'He'll give you much more scope. I think you're ready for it. I would like Jonathan to have that sort of horse—' She paused and frowned at the thought of Jonathan, and changed the subject. 'Well, I hope you'll soon be up and about again, Peter. It's just concussion, I take it? Nothing broken?'

'No.' He didn't offer to show her the bruises, but sank back into his pillow, looking remarkably ill.

'I'm so sorry, Peter.' She looked genuinely sympathetic this time. 'I do want you to ride in our team this summer—' (or was it just self-interest, Ruth wondered)—'and come to camp as well. You could be so much help. Gary Major is coming to instruct, and we want to get a tetrathlon team going.'

'I want to come to camp,' Peter said. 'I'd like to. And the team. On Sirius.'

'Ah, well, we'll have to talk to your father. I'm glad you want to come.' She got up, looking kindly again, and sympathetic. 'Get better quickly then. I'm so glad it wasn't any worse.'

She patted his hand in a motherly way and departed, leaving the three of them considering the manipulations of the adult mind. Peter suddenly looked much better.

'What's camp like?' asked Thea.

'It's good if you get a decent instructor,' Peter said. 'Gary Major is okay. And some one decent to share a caravan with. If Jonathan is coming—and I don't suppose he stands a chance of not—I'll be okay there. They've got a plushy caravan too. Running hot.'

'Are you going?' Thea asked Ruth.

'Yes. I haven't got a plushy caravan though. Only a tent.'

'Could I share with you?'

'Yes, of course.'

'We could use the trailer to sleep in, if the tent isn't big enough. Where do they have it?'

'Maybridge. It's a farm, the Hunt Sec.'s farm. Very remote and rustic. No mod. cons. at all, apart from the running hot in the

Meredith caravan. No pub within walking distance. Spartan.'

'Sounds nice,' Thea said. 'Just what I'm used to.'

Ruth was wondering whether Peter knew that he wasn't going to be allowed to ride Sirius any more. Had his father told him, or was he going to tactfully wean Peter off Sirius by offering him Solomon's Seal instead? But it would hardly be tactful to ask. Peter's attitude towards her was still cool, and he spoke mostly to Thea. Ruth, hurt but not surprised, was glad when the visit was over.

'THIS team—' Mrs. Meredith let out a groan, riffling through her card index. 'I've rashly entered a team, but when it comes to declaring it—' She gave a shrug. 'I had such hopes.'

'And what's happened to them?' Jonathan asked, humouring her.

'There's Thea and Bright Morning. They're all right. Apart from them, nothing but problems. You, for example, haven't ridden Railway to the best of my knowledge for at least a fortnight. How you expect him to perform—'

'It's all this homework,' Jonathan said, annoyed at being attacked when he had been all prepared to be sympathetic.

'Oh, rubbish. You have plenty of time to listen to all those dreadful records in your room. However—' Perhaps she thought it wasn't fair too, for she switched. 'No doubt he'll go all right, especially as we have a week at camp just beforehand. You and Thea I am depending on. After that, well—'

'Peter.'

'Who on?'

'His new one. What's it called? Or Sirius.'

'Sirius is out at grass over at Maybridge, abandoned, as far as I can make out. Peter is not allowed to have any more to do with him. He's got this new one, Solomon, it's true, but I've since found out that the horse was bought with a client already in mind, and as soon as it's going well, it's going to be sold. Typical McNair. He made out to me that it was for Peter. It is a good one, true, but how can you count on McNair not to sell it before the Area Trials? He says he won't, and he says Peter will be bringing it to camp, but you can't rely on that man. So Peter is down with a question mark.'

'And how about our Ruthie?'

'That's the biggest question mark of all. That pony is a real handful for her. Its dressage test is hair-raising, and it's likely to demolish the show-jumping ring completely. It won a first at that show where Peter nearly killed himself, and since then it's knocked everything down. Or so I gather. That child needs help. I really think we'll have to have a full-scale dress rehearsal and see how this famous team makes out under the proper competition conditions. There's a One-Day Event at Pickworth in the middle of June. I think I'll enter you four and see what happens. I've got the schedules somewhere—' She started scrummaging through her desk. 'Would you like to ring them up for me, and see if it's all right for dates—nobody doing anything else? We'll pay the fees out of funds, and lay on the transport.'

'Okay.'

Jonathan tried not to show the heart-sinking he felt at the prospect, being in a co-operative mood. It wasn't that he minded the riding; in fact, the cross-country courses were fine and bombing over big jumps on the redoubtable Railwayman was an exhilarating and satisfying way of spending time—the trouble was, unlike the other three members of the team, he had no competitive spirit. He didn't want to prove anything to anybody, either about himself or his horse. And the events undoubtedly attracted the competitive. They thronged with sharp-eyed parents with stop-watches and exhortations, and dedicated riders disputing the best line through a particular hazard, the most advantageous angle of approach, the possibilities of bonus points. The technicalities of it all bored him stiff, and he disliked the formality of the dressage test, and having to be impeccably turned out, and the waiting around, and some of the people were horrible. . . .

'You don't look very keen', his mother said. He sensed the accusation. 'Oh—no, it's all right—'

He moved over to the telephone, and sat on the old Jacobean chest which served as a telephone seat, and dialled Peter's number. Peter was quite agreeable, and so was Thea. He moved on to Ruth.

'It's Jonathan Meredith. I've got a proposition for you.'

'Oh!'

The obvious surprise was followed by an anticipatory silence which frightened Jonathan into realizing that the remark was perhaps unfortunately worded: he hurried on, 'If you're not doing anything on June the thirtieth, mother wants to enter you for a One-Day Event at Pickworth. We're all going—Peter and Thea and me. A sort of practice. I take it you're game?'

'Oh, golly, does she really want me?'

'So she said.'

Another silence. A nervous muttering. 'Oh, golly.'

Jonathan said kindly, 'Transport laid on, fees paid. Absolutely nothing to worry about.'

'That's what you think.' Another contemplative silence. 'I haven't got a crash-helmet. Or a black jacket.'

'You can borrow Jessica's.'

'I'm no good at the dressage—'

'No. None of us are. Don't let that put you off. You're coming? Yes? Of course.'

'If you say so.'

'Fine. Done. Committed. Cheerio.'

He put the receiver down and grinned at his mother. 'All laid on. Black Saturday, as far as Ruth is concerned—but it'll be all right on the day.'

'God help us, I hope so.'

12

RUTH sought Thea out at school.

'Did Jonathan ring you up yesterday? About Pickworth.'

'Yes.' Thea smiled. 'You're going, aren't you? He said you and Peter.'

'I said yes, but I'm terrified.'

'Well, you're daft. To be terrified. You exaggerate. You're slightly nervous that you might not demonstrate your obvious potential as well as you would like to. That apprehension afflicts us all. Even our Peter. Talking of Peter, a very strange thing happened last night.'

'What was that?'

'I took Morning out for an hour, and I was riding down that track that goes through the bottom of Maybridge woods, and I saw Peter—riding Sirius.'

Ruth stared. 'You never! He's forbidden—there was the most colossal row about it.'

'I know. Peter told me. He's not to ride Sirius under any circumstances—they had a right old bust-up, from what I gather.'

'And Sirius was sent down to Maybridge, out of the way. You mean Peter goes down there and rides him without father McNair knowing?' Ruth's voice was full of awe at the thought. 'I'd call that risky.'

'More from father McNair than Sirius, you mean? So would I. He didn't see me.'

'What was he doing?'

'Just riding round the field. Schooling.'

'Crikey! Have you said anything to him?'

'No. I haven't seen him today. I don't think we ought to say anything, do you? I bet he wouldn't want us to know.'

'No. We could ask him if he's going to Pickworth though, and who he's riding. Just friendly like. See if he says anything.'

'Okay.'

It was lunch-time, and Peter's year was milling about in its characteristically aimless fashion waiting for the bell to go. There was no sign of Peter.

'He ought to be there. Sanders is there, and Monkton.' They were Peter's friends.

'We can ask them.'

They did. Sanders and Monkton looked slightly cagey. 'McNair? Have you seen McNair, Monkton?'

'Can't say as I have, Sanders.'

'No, can't say as I have either, Monkton.'

'Do you know where he is?' Ruth persisted.

'I might know, but then I might not be saying, might I?' Monkton said.

'He *ought* to be here,' Ruth said.

'You're forgetting,' Sanders said. 'We've got games all afternoon, and our McNair's got a sore head. Little argument with a nag, we understand. McNair doesn't play games any more. He's got a useful letter from a doctor to say no games.'

'Ah.' Ruth began to sense what they were getting at. 'Then he works in the library instead?' That was the usual practice if one was excused games.

'Could be. Could be.'

But when the bell had gone, there was no sign of Peter in the library, nor anywhere else. Ruth and Thea began to see the light.

'What a very useful set-up!' Thea pointed out. 'If you're trusted to work in the library, unsupervised, every games afternoon—which is nearly every afternoon if you're in the teams, which Peter is—and Maybridge is fifteen minutes away by bicycle—'

'Do you think he does, really?'

'Yes, I do. And any odd evening, if he can get away. It's just the sort of thing he would do.'

'Yes, it fits.' Ruth agreed, remembering Peter's agonized plea to save Sirius from his father's wrath. Although Sirius had been spared the bullet, it was no life for a creature of his spirit to be turned out alone in a distant field to rot, as Peter would be the first to appreciate.

'But I wonder what's the point of it all?' Thea said curiously. 'Just to nark his father? Or does he really want that badly to have Sirius make good?'

Ruth, looking out of the corridor window on to a summer field fringed with elm, and the lane dipping away towards the next valley and the quiet woods that fringed the Maybridge estate (in the other direction the lane was concreted and led directly into the large village of Hanningham from which the school took its name) knew exactly what the point was, but couldn't put it into words. She stopped, and gazed out of the window. A great envy of Peter engulfed her—that he had both the nerve and ability to go hammering away at the thing he stubbornly wanted, despite all obstacles: he went his way like a bulldozer, completely on his own, wanting nothing of anybody. It might be that, almost more than what he was actually doing. His own way, the right to assert his independence. She knew how he felt with an almost desperate sympathy, and stared towards the distant woods with a strange feeling of her spirit having departed completely from Hanningham Comprehensive and followed the dipping lane after Peter's . . .

13

THERE were rooks nesting in the woods, and they went up on huge black wings with their raucous summer voices, wheeling against the sky. Peter coasted down the last hill, humming to the whirr of his wheels, watching the rooks, feeling possessed of such freedom that it made him feel almost intoxicated. With his doctor's letter and the lovely secrecy of the Maybridge farm with its strange little hills and the running streams, enormous flowering hedges, and brooding woods, and the gorgeous, evil Sirius awaiting him, dusty with pollen, swollen with summer grass, it was like a story-book existence, leaving the everyday, the smell of chalk and footballs and not very clean lavatories, and going through the fairy-book door into another whole world. Peter didn't care for school, and very little for bookwork and his O-level prospects. It was as if the bump on his head had opened his eyes to what a drudge he was, toeing the line, eternally slaving for his father. Seeing Toad again had set something off in him. He didn't know quite what it was, only that, setting eyes on him again, he had felt stirrings of an unimaginable pain, a fierce longing for something he felt he had once shared with that pony when Toad had been fresh from his mountains and amidst his great confusion and bewilderment amongst his new harsh experiences had seemed—or so it had appeared to Peter at the time—to put a peculiar trust in him. Peter at the same time had wanted something to sink his own despondencies in. They had come together through a mutual need. Seeing him again in the snowy darkness, after Ruth's telephone call, he had remembered with extraordinary clarity the urgent feelings that had underlain his partnership with Toad. The horsy people had all said that they were 'a great combination'. In their hearty, heartless way they had recognized the partnership, but nothing of the reasons why. His father had understood nothing, else he would never have sold him on. Peter, realizing now, hadn't realized at the time either. It was only now, with a pattern apparently being repeated, that he was experienced enough to sense what had happened before.

'But this time—' he said out loud, 'this time is different—' This time he was much tougher, and this time he didn't *need* Sirius. This time Sirius was merely an excuse. It was true that he had a very

strong sympathy with the animal, but it was more than that: Sirius was a rebel, banished, and joining him Peter felt a marvellous release, a rebel himself. He didn't like school; he was always rowing with his father; he never seemed to be getting anywhere at all, for he was always slaving away at things he didn't like; he didn't know what he wanted; but he had discovered, the very first time he had handed over the doctor's letter, sat bored in the library for five minutes and then thought of this marvellous escape, that the afternoons he spent at Maybridge were completely happy. He wasn't, after all, a great rebel; it was all on a fairly harmless scale. But the lovely solitude, and the challenge of the difficult animal which was something he understood and enjoyed, and the complete freedom to work in his own way, at his own pace, soothed his discontented spirit astonishingly. There was nothing to regret down here, seeing Sirius come to meet him along his own trodden track, his nostrils rippling a greeting. It was a world of its own. No one to interfere, no one even to see. Even without Sirius at all, it would have been a perfect rest-cure. But boring fairly soon, probably. Sirius gave it all a reason.

'Don't you, my nag? My reason in life. Taming your bloody great psychological hang-ups.'

Other people played truant to go fishing, or ride their motor bikes. He played truant to ride Sirius. It was perfectly straight-forward. He even thought, having got used to it, that it was neces-sary to him. If he was discovered, he would have to use his con-cussion to explain his wayward behaviour. He had a reputation for waywardness, after all—although, considering his circumstances, he had always considered that his behaviour had been perfectly logical and consistent. Try to get *them* to see that—

'That's another matter, isn't it?' Peter spoke to Sirius as he brushed him over, and put on his saddle and bridle which he kept up on the rafters of the barn in the field. His voice soothed the pony, who stood quietly, flicking one ear back. Peter couldn't remember feeling so happy for years. He mounted, and rode away down the field.

14

RUTH had looked up the address of the man who had bought Fly-by-Night in the telephone book, and resolved to ride over to have a look at the pony's living conditions. Glutton for punishment that she was, she didn't suppose the expedition would give her any cause for joy, but she felt a responsibility for the situation. She could not shut her mind to it. With Ted's strictures still in mind, she determined not to make another scene, only to look, passing by, and under no circumstances to knock at the door and make rude accusations, whatever the provocation. She mustn't be childish. At this thought, her heart gave a great leap of pure funk at the recollection of Jonathan's telephone call, and she made a fervent vow never again to say, 'Oh, golly, I can't!' and suchlike childish and unworthy protestations, especially to Jonathan. Even Thea was getting fed up with her. She supposed that even Jonathan and Thea had doubts, setting off on a cross-country with the honour of the Pony Club at stake, but they didn't go round telling everyone. 'I must keep quiet and calm and dignified,' she vowed. She was the youngest and most inexperienced of this embryo team, but it didn't mean she had to act like it all the time. Tedious for the others, who had problems as well. All the same, she dreaded Pickworth, and had a large black ring round it on her calendar.

Toad was now very fit and strong, and even hacking she couldn't relax and gaze at the lovely countryside, as he was apt to take off if he saw a nice grass verge, or if they got amongst exciting, rustling trees, or saw an unexpected bicycle appear from a side road. Ruth knew that her riding had improved no end, but rather suspected that Toad would always be one jump ahead of her; she could cope, but whether she would ever succeed she doubted. No, she mustn't doubt. She must determine. She tightened her knees and shortened her reins and Toad went eagerly into his springing trot, lifting up his knees and curving his neck. He covered the ground at a great pace, even when collected; a good method of transport by any reckoning. He covered the five miles to Fly's new home in under half an hour. The house was a new bungalow on the edge of a village. Ruth intended just to ride by, without stopping, but the road was a cul-de-sac, which made it a bit awkward. She didn't want to get cornered by the unpleasant man, but with luck he would be at work; in fact, with luck they would all be at work and she could have a good nose. She turned Toad up the road and made him walk slowly, feeling apprehensive. She couldn't believe that it could possibly be all right, that she would find Fly happily grazing in a beautifully-kept field with a spotless water-trough and a nice little shed for shade. For a moment, one lovely fleeting moment, she thought she might, when she first caught sight of the bungalow and its garden, both very tidy and well-tended, with smart paint, and rows of bedding plants in primary colours, and no sign at all of not being able to afford anything (which she always privately thought her own homes had always suffered from) —but then, from her vantage point on Toad, she was able to see over the neatly trimmed privet on the far side of the garden, and take in a very small, bare strip of grazing, with rusty barbed wire marking it off from a field of young corn. It had no shed and no shelter and the water was in an old bath, and Fly was standing up at the far end, resting one leg in a dispirited fashion. Ruth pulled up, forgetting about not being seen, but unfortunately it was too late, for Fly had heard Toad. He put up his head and let out a piercing whinny and came galloping down the field in a cloud of dust. He trotted up and down the awful wire, head up, still whinnying, and Ruth could see at close quarters his staring coat and rubbed flanks, his sad deterioration from the days in her lush field, when she had always had a job not to let him get too fat. Not caring about anything else, Ruth rode up close and gave him the last crumby bits of pony-nuts she had in her jeans pocket, and then turned round and rode blindly away, his sad whinnying behind her, caged in his beastly little field, rending all her brave resolutions into bits. She wept bitterly all the way home, and Toad's swinging pace and jaunty manners gave her no joy at all, bought at such expense. She felt like a traitor, after all the happiness Fly had given her, to land him in such a state, yet she was quite powerless now to deliver him. She had no money even should the man be willing to sell him back.

She went over to Thea's and wept copiously in the dim, evening cavern of Bright Morning's barn, sitting on the feed-bin and crushing corn-husks between her nails like fleas, while Thea brushed her pony over and tacked him up. She did not expect Thea to come up with a solution, for there wasn't one.

'Even if I save—and anyway, I can't, because it all goes on keeping Toad—there just isn't any way at all—'

'No. Only perhaps if you know someone else who would buy him. If the man wants to sell him anyway. He probably doesn't. If you really can't do anything, which you can't, the best thing is to forget it. It'll only make you miserable, to no avail at all. After all, he's not actually starving or getting beaten up. It's all relative, how ponies are treated. Most of them aren't treated nearly as well as ours, but they're all right.'

Even Thea knew it was cold comfort, guessing only too well how Ruth felt.

'It's no good being sentimental,' she said, but from the tone of her voice it was clear that she knew it wasn't sentiment. Just for something to say.

'Come and jump Toad. He'll go like a bomb and cheer you up. It won't get you anywhere, carrying on over Fly.'

Toad did go like a bomb, but it didn't cheer Ruth up. She didn't cheer up for several days. If Fly was like that now, in the summer, whatever must he have been like all through the winter, when the field would just have been mud? He couldn't possibly stay there another winter, even if she had to steal him, which wouldn't be difficult with only that miserable bit of wire to cut through. Ruth considered the possibilities, then remembered that she was a new, improved, adult Ruth, and not given any more to childish ideas, and stealing Fly wasn't really in line with her new image. Perhaps, if she was successful with Toad in the team and Mrs. Meredith was nice to her, she could ask her for help again. The Merediths were supposed to be vastly rich, and buying Fly-by-Night couldn't possibly upset their way of life to any great degree. The woman must realize, if she had any soul at all, how miserable the situation was, and how guilty it made her feel.

Being successful in the team was a problem all on its own, of course. Before Pickworth, she took Toad to two small shows, and at each one he knocked jumps down because she could not keep him steady enough and present him correctly. But at least he didn't disgrace her, and his faults as usual were caused by impetuosity, which was not to be deprecated—only handled with the proper skill. At Pickworth there would be a dressage test, a show-jumping competition and a cross-country: Ruth guessed that he was most likely to shine in the cross-country, if he was destined to shine at all, for that is what he had always done so superbly with Peter, but as she had never done a full-sized proper cross-country with him yet—only small Pony Club rally efforts—she felt unable to consider even that part of the day with any confidence.

She had even less cause for confidence by the time the day arrived, for beside the large black ring she had put round the date on the calendar there was a smaller mark, an ominous little star which she used for the more common and mundane problems of her life. Sure enough, when she woke up on the morning of the fated day, she felt terrible, heavy and tired and sick, and with a miserable stomach-ache, all the familiar symptoms of starting the curse. She lay in bed staring at the ceiling, possessed of a black, diabolical humour. As if she didn't have enough against her! The room was grey, and through the window she could see cool, unsummer-like clouds in great heaps across the sky and the elms threshing their heavy green heads sullenly, as if in league with some celestial conspiracy against her. It had been raining, and was obviously going to rain again.

'I don't care,' she thought, 'it doesn't matter. It's good for the character.' But the character was at low ebb, and at breakfast she sat white and pinched-looking, so that her mother took one look and recognized the situation immediately.

'Not much good your going in that state!'

'I'll have to,' Ruth said. 'It'll go off. I'll take some aspirins.'

Her mother shrugged, pursing her lips. She put the aspirin bottle on the table. She knew, for the whole family could hardly have been unaware, how much this day meant to Ruth.

'It takes an hour and a half to get there,' Ruth said. 'I'll be all right by then, I can doze off in the horse-box. And the weather will have cleared too. It will be all right.'

Fortunately she had ridden Toad over to Merediths' the day before, and had given him a good grooming and left all her things there ready. Her father was going to drop her there on his way to work. She forced some breakfast down, to placate her mother rather than because she wanted to, and her mother made her some sandwiches and put them in a basket.

'You really have got everything?'

There was so much in the way of clothes, jeans and old things for going in, a jersey and crash-helmet for the cross-country, black jacket, tie and black hat for the dressage, a parka because it was going to be cold and wet—she had sorted them all out and had the things she wasn't wearing in plastic bags.

'I mustn't forget the things I've got to borrow off Jessica too.' But she didn't really feel all there. She hoped Mrs. Meredith would organize her. . . .

'Well, it's a quarter to eight. You'd better be off. Do look after yourself.'

If Ruth had been in a discerning mood she would have noticed that her mother looked worried to death. She got into the car with her father, with all her things piled on the back seat, and they drove over to the Merediths'. Ruth's one determination was not to look ill before they were safely away in the horse-box, unless Mrs. Meredith decided to take Jessica and Cuthbert instead, so when she unloaded she made hearty good-mornings to every one in sight and set about giving Toad a quick brushing over and getting him ready. There was so much to do, bandaging and loading up and getting hay-nets filled and remembering buckets and sweat-rugs and Jessica's hat and jacket that she did in fact forget her state of health, and it didn't come back to her until they were ready to leave and Mrs. Meredith told them to hurry up and pile in, else they wouldn't have time to walk the course.

'Mrs. Towler's sitting in front with me, and Jim's coming as well, so you children had better all travel in the back. Up you go!'

Mrs. Towler was the Pony Club Secretary. Mrs. Meredith was

driving, and there was only room for three in the cab, so it was quite normal for the riders to travel with the horses in the groom's compartment. Normally Ruth would not have minded, but as soon as she settled herself on the floor against a hay-net with her back to the engine, a view of pony's legs before her and a smell of dung and diesel fuel in her nostrils, she felt doomed. Two black jackets on hangers swung to and fro in front of her nose and Peter sat squashed hard against her eating bacon sandwiches which didn't help at all. He was riding Solomon, whose legs Ruth was now regarding. Not a word about Sirius. Ruth tried to think about Sirius, and the interesting Peter situation, to take her mind off her troubles, but as she didn't feel brave enough to question Peter about it, the few thoughts didn't occupy her for very long. She began to feel very sick, and the pains in her stomach increased with the vibration of the lorry. They had fifty miles to go. After twenty, she said weakly to Peter, 'Is there a bucket handy?'

'Oh, gawd,' said Peter. There was a hurried scrabble round, and Jonathan banged on the window into the cab and Mrs. Meredith drew into the next lay-by. Ruth was transferred to the cab, and Jim relegated to the back. She sat between the two women trying to look as if she was recovering, but it was quite impossible. As the countryside reeled past, she felt herself reeling with it. Mrs. Towler found a cushion for her head, and made sure the bucket was handy and made motherly noises at her side, and Ruth lapsed into a semi-doze. But even in a partly unconscious state, she could not help being aware that Mrs. Meredith was very annoyed, however sympathetic Mrs. Towler might be.

By the time they arrived, the weather had cleared slightly and a hesitant sun was making exploratory forays over the ancient oaks of Pickworth Park, shining invitingly on the acres of deer-grazed grass. Mrs. Meredith parked in the horse-lines, switched off the engine, and turned to Ruth.

'Well, how are we? Walking the course might do a lot of good. Do you feel up to it? I'll go and get your numbers and see if they're running to time.'

Ruth lifted her head and looked at the scene, which was very professional-looking, a miniature Badminton, with plenty of impeccably turned-out ponies already in action over by the dressage arena, and an efficient loud-speaker system calling out names. The jumps in the show-jumping area gleamed in the sunshine, very bright and formidable. Ruth felt desperately sick. If only she could walk the course, she could be sick amongst the oak trees where no one would see.

'Yes,' she said.

Thea came to fetch her, kind and anxious. 'Here's your parka. We're all going. You'll probably feel all right in the fresh air.'

'Shall I bring the bucket?' Peter asked.

'Oh, shut up,' Thea said angrily.

The four of them set off, scuffing over the smooth turf, hunched into old anoraks, to see the perils Pickworth had to offer. Ruth doubted if it would make her feel any better.

'It's generally nice here,' Jonathan was saying. 'Big and fast and not too tricksy.'

Ruth could picture him on the bold Railwayman, sitting there and not bothering; in spite of his mother, he didn't seem to care whether he did well or not. He had a completely untroubled confidence. Peter, never having ridden his new point-to-point horse in a competition before, seemed similarly untroubled. Ruth was deeply envious. Thea kept close to her, kindly and sympathetic, and Ruth tried to dredge up reserves of courage and fire which she doubted existed.

It seemed to her a very long way. She was aware of red and white flags and massive telegraph poles blocking large ditches, of an enormous fallen tree with an ambulance parked malevolently beside it, of lovely soft galloping ground through the oak woods, with sporadic obstacles such as a pile of cut timber, a stiff flight of railway sleepers, a wide ditch with rails on the far side, a running stream with a cruel drop in, and a long scramble out up a gravel embankment. Coming back out of the woods to face the last leg up to the finish, she felt unaccountably weak at the knees.

'I say, are you all right?' Jonathan, looking back, stopped suddenly and put out an arm. Ruth fell on it gratefully, the sky seeming to have come down on her head. She was aware of the smell of damp turf in her nostrils, and the sudden concern in Jonathan's eyes, which warmed her even as she passed out. Some one came down in a car and collected her, and she next became coherent lying on the seat in the front of the horse-box with Mrs. Meredith grimly sponging her face with cold water, as if she was a horse.

'It's not nerves, I hope?' she was saying briskly.

'It's the curse. I'll be all right soon.'

'You certainly won't be riding in this condition, my girl. I wouldn't like to be responsible. You must just keep warm and rest.'

'But the team—'

'It's the best three out of four. We can still compete. It just means the others mustn't make mistakes. There's no need for you to worry.'

She said it with such ferocity that Ruth did not dare speak again. The horse-box was crashing and resounding to the sound of the ponies being unboxed. Ruth felt a great pang for Toad, unable to compete, left tied up alone while the others went prancing away, and a self-pity that almost overwhelmed her. A crash more violent than all the others and a shriek from the ramp sent Mrs. Meredith scurrying abruptly from her side to see what was happening. It was the usual panic, Ruth presumed, trying to get ready in time. She heard Peter shout something, and then Jonathan reply, obviously het up about something, and Mrs. Meredith's despairing, 'You imbeciles! Are you quite incapable—!'

Whatever it was, she was not the only one in trouble. She was filled with despair at her helplessness, and shut her eyes and presumably dozed off for when she came to again it was all quiet. Everyone had departed. She sat up muzzily and looked out of the window. There seemed to be plenty of people about, and spectators cars surrounding the show-jumping arena, but no sign of her own party. She felt very thirsty, and decided to get up and fetch her provisions from the groom's department, and see what she felt like on her feet.

She felt decidedly weak, but no longer sick and dizzy. It was even worse, feeling better, than being too ill to care. Nothing was going to make the day other than total disaster, so she tried to make her mind a blank, climbing up into the lorry and hunting round for her bottle of lemonade. She found it and sat on a hay-net. The lorry was quiet, like a big cave, smelling of straw and manure and no longer of diesel fumes. She considered it for a few minutes, and then realized that Toad wasn't there. He had been the inside pony, and she would have thought they would have left him undisturbed. She looked outside, to see if he was tied up outside, but he wasn't. She sat back on the hay-net again, and had another swig of lemonade, and tried to think of a logical reason for Toad not being there, but she couldn't.

'There must be a reason,' she thought. It was her state of health, preventing her from seeing sense.

Whilst she was occupied with these thoughts, Jonathan appeared, climbing up through the little door.

'Oh, hullo,' he said cheerfully. 'Feel better?'

'Yes, a bit.'

He looked fantastically smart and unfamiliar in his black jacket and boots with spurs.

'Have you done the dressage?'

'Yes, and the show-jumping.'

'How did you do?'

'I did clear in the show-jumping. The dressage felt pretty ghastly—it always does—but could have been worse. He was pulling like a train all through it, all overbent and lots of tail-twitching, but we did mostly do the right things at the right markers, so it could have been worse.'

'What about the others?'

'Thea hasn't gone yet. Peter's show-jumping. I've got to change for the cross-country—chuck me that hanger, will you?'

Ruth got the impression that he was being cagey about something, almost as if he was nervous of her, in a hurry to be away. She didn't see how he could possibly know how much she liked him, as she had been superlatively careful to give no hint at all; she even looked away, now, politely, as he stripped off his tie and shirt, instead of gazing avidly at his rippling muscles; however, he then couldn't find his jersey and spent ages hunting about half-naked, and in the end she had to help him, and had plenty of time to take in his wiry torso and commendable biceps before discovering the jersey wrapped up in a ball inside the bundle that was Railway's sweat-rug. He pulled it on, muttering thanks, and while he was still inside it she said, 'What have you done with Toad?'

His head came out of the top, the curls springing out extravagantly. He didn't reply, shrugging his arms through the sleeves. She thought he hadn't heard, so she repeated the question. He reached for his crash-helmet, which they had discovered earlier when looking for the jersey, and put it on, squashing most of the hair up inside it.

'Mother gets mad at hair,' he said.

'Where's Toad?' she said again.

He gave her a funny look, which she couldn't understand at all and said, 'You'd better ask Peter. It was none of my doing, believe me. I was all against it, without asking you.'

'Without asking me what?'

'Toad, I mean, and Peter. But we were entered as a team, that was the trouble. Solomon came off the ramp when we were unboxing, and cut himself on the hock. Quite deep. Dead duck—just like you. So mother decided, rather than have no team to enter, to put Peter on Toad. And that's where Toad is.'

'You mean show-jumping with Peter?'

'Yes, I'm afraid so.'

Ruth had no words. She felt struck down, almost physically, by Jonathan's information. Just like before, when Peter had ridden him for a couple of practice jumps, but now, in the whole event . . . it was almost more than she could take.

'It's this team thing, you see.' Jonathan was looking very earnest. 'You're always lumbered—sinking personal glory for the common good, and all that rot. I'm only warning you what you'll get from mother, if you protest. The way it worked out, one rider and one horse incapacitated, whichever it had been, she'd have done the same. It might have landed up with you on Railway, or me on Bright Morning—it's just your luck it had to be this way round.'

Looking at Jonathan, and seeing that he was terrified she was going to burst into tears and that he, to use his own term, was going to be 'lumbered', she remembered her new image and Ted's admonitions and said, 'I'll come down to the start with you. I'm not so sickly that I can't watch.'

Jonathan smiled gratefully and handed her tenderly down out of the horse-box, obviously not aware that she desperately wanted to throw herself into his desirable maroon and pale-blue arms and weep herself into oblivion. It was amazing how easy it was to deceive, Ruth discovered, if one was firm enough. She felt grim and deathly and wild with rage and frustration, but found she was walking calmly at Jonathan's side and listening politely to his doubts about Railway going into the water without kicking up a fuss, and presumably looking quite normal, for no one gave them a second glance. I ought to be an actress, Ruth thought.

In the cross-country collecting ring they found Thea holding Railway.

'You know what's happened, I suppose?' she said. 'Has Jonathan told you?'

'Yes. It doesn't matter.' Ruth was beginning to get interested in her new powers. 'It would have been stupid to withdraw.'

Thea looked surprised. 'Yes, of course. That's what we all thought, but—' She exchanged a glance with Jonathan which Ruth noted. She said to Jonathan, 'Your mother's tied up with Solomon and the vet. She said if we wanted her—'

'We don't,' Jonathan said. It occurred to Ruth that perhaps having 'professional' parents, like Jonathan and Peter, was more of a disadvantage than she had realised, for ever being exhorted to greater things, one's inefficiencies a cause for grief; she certainly had not noticed a loving dependency in either of the boys' attitudes, but rather a relationship summed up by Jonathan's terse, 'I'd rather go round without her seeing. I know where I go wrong, without her telling me.'

'Here's Peter now. If he's finished jumping, I'm four after him. I'd better go.'

Toad came up at a trot, overbending slightly and looking very cocky. Peter saw Ruth and pulled up, his animation clouding abruptly into an obvious apprehension.

'What did you do?' Jonathan shouted. 'Clear?'

'Yes.'

If he had been eliminated at the first jump, Ruth knew that she would have felt a lot better, but she very carefully looked cheerful. Peter said to her, 'He went beautifully.' He slid off and started to loosen the girths. Ruth took Toad's rein and scratched his nose where he liked it, not daring to say anything, in spite of her resolution. Peter, not looking at her, said, 'This wasn't my idea, you know. Mrs. Meredith decided.'

'I know. You don't mind though?' Ruth couldn't help being catty, and regretted it immediately.

'I'd rather ride him than Solomon,' Peter said. 'But I'd rather have ridden Sirius than either of them.' He sounded aggressive. He straightened up. 'I suppose you're furious? I couldn't help it, you know.'

It was as near an apology as he was capable of. Ruth said, 'I know. It's all right.'

He smiled. For a moment Ruth felt that they were almost on the old footing, but the pressures of the day did not allow for the niceties of relation-building, for he then said, 'I've got to go and change for the cross-country. Will you hold him?'

'Yes.'

He went back to the horse-box, and Ruth climbed on to Toad and rode down to watch Thea in the show-jumping ring. She too got a clear round. She came out grinning and Jonathan rode up and they exchanged notes on their respective rounds while Ruth sat and listened. Their mutual bond, the heightened excitement in their manner and the way they spoke made Ruth even more aware of what she was missing: this was the team spirit working in its most satisfying way, the possibility of success forging a stronger and more intimate association; she felt extraordinarily cut off, in a sense more hurt by missing this experience than by the purely personal hurt of Peter riding Toad. Jonathan perhaps realized this, for when Thea had ridden away to get changed, and they were walking Toad and Railway round the collecting-ring side by side, he said to her, 'It's a great pity for you, today. Missing it. If it had been me, I'd have been quite pleased. But you want to.'

'Yes.' She was feeling better every minute, but it was too late now. Fatal to let her mind dwell on her fate. Switch to Jonathan's revelation. 'You don't like it?'

'Well, I'm looking forward to going round now, this minute. But on the whole I don't like competitions. Doing it in public. It all seems a bit pointless.'

'You've done too many? You're bored? My trouble is I don't know if I can even get round. I still won't know after today.'

'You would. Of course you would. Toad's going splendidly. It's your spade-work. It doesn't just happen.'

Ruth wished she could believe him. Jonathan had the knack of saying the reassuring thing, as if he really understood; he cared about other people's feelings. He was kind and sensitive in the nicest possible way. And if he didn't mean what he was saying he was—like her—a very good actor.

'Number eighty-eight! You're next to go.'

That was Jonathan. He pulled up and tightened his girths a hole and grimaced at Ruth.

'Wish me luck!'

'Oh, of course!'

Railwayman, aware of what was in store for him, was suddenly all springs, and yawing at his bit. Jonathan's expression changed, looking down towards the start, holding the pony in hard. He looked very confident and determined, in spite of what he had said a moment earlier, and was away at an instant gallop the moment the flag fell.

There was a good view of quite a lot of the course from the side of the hill by the start and finish, and one could estimate the speed of progress by how long the competitor remained out of sight in the various belts of woodland. Some disappeared never to be seen again; several got into trouble at a nasty in-and-out on the far hillside, and the water was reputed to be causing trouble, although it was out of sight from where Ruth was. Ruth, on her vantage point from Toad's back, saw Railway take the first three jumps at a cracking pace and disappear from view into the oak wood, from which he emerged in phenomenally quick time to go belting up to the in-and-out. This Railway accomplished without any trouble, turning sharply to head down to the water, and disappearing out of sight again. At this point Peter returned, wearing a bright orange jersey and clashing red silk.

'How are we doing?'

'Okay so far. He's at the water.'

'Railway doesn't like water.'

'Oh—well, he's made it. There he is!'

They watched the distant horse and rider travelling across the opposite hillside at hair-raising speed, take a large hedge in their stride and turn down the hill towards the big ditch at the bottom and the uphill finish.

'God, that horse can travel,' Peter remarked. 'You wouldn't think so, to look at it. I bet that's the fastest round today.'

'If Thea's done a clear, we're doing—you're doing quite well,' Ruth said. 'So far, anyway.'

'Toad should go round—oh, cripes! Jonathan!' Railway was going so fast that he carried away the rails across the ditch. He came through the finish as if he was all set to go round again, and Jonathan had considerable difficulty in pulling up. He came back to them, grinning, holding Railway in hard. The roan cob was quite dry and hardly breathing any more heavily than when he set off. Jonathan was covered in mud, pleased and excited.

'Five faults for those bloody rails! He was clear apart from that. Nearly had me off at the water though. He pecked, and I thought I was going to have to swim for it, then he chucked his head up and pushed me back in the saddle again. Nearly broke my nose—better than drowning though.'

Ruth got off Toad, feeling inferior, like a groom. Peter lengthened the stirrups and felt the girth and Jonathan told him what to look out for, and Thea came back from the show-jumping ring to announce that she had gone clear.

'I say, we're in with a chance, if you don't do anything bloody stupid,' Jonathan said to Peter. 'There hasn't been a clear round yet.' Ruth got the job of riding Bright Morning round while Thea went to change, and Jonathan rode beside her again, cooling off Railway. They both watched Peter ride down to the start, and circle, waiting for his flag. Ruth could not take her eyes off Toad, curvetting with anticipation, a little flame-coloured charger. Now that she was reconciled, she felt imbued with a curious excitement, ready to see Toad go round and feel that she was involved, almost as if she was doing it herself, but without the awful responsibility.

She was almost relieved, the way things had worked out, and yet appalled at feeling relieved. Watching Peter, it was doing it by proxy. When the flag fell, and he went straight into a gallop and away over the soft turf to the first jump, she remembered vividly the first time she had set eyes on Peter and Toad, doing exactly the same thing, and how she had admired the combination, even then recognizing the perfect *rapport* between the pair, although she had known nothing about horses or trials or one-day-events or anything else at the time—now, watching them again, she was so intimately involved that it was as if she was ghost-riding for Peter, feeling Toad, enjoying Peter's skill, Peter's judgement, pretending they were her own, pretending that, had all been well, Toad would have done exactly this for her. Would he? How would she ever know? They did a clear round twenty seconds slower than Jonathan. Ruth was screwed up with her proxy achievement, not knowing whether to laugh or cry, Jonathan was smiling again, excited.

'He was splendid! A lovely round—'

'But—'

'Oh, Ruth!' Jonathan spared her, even in the mounting excitement, his rare sympathy—'He would have gone the same for you! Why ever do you think he wouldn't?'

Mrs. Meredith appeared at this point, obviously pleased and hopeful, and said, 'You stand quite a good chance of getting somewhere, if Thea keeps it up. You were second in the dressage, Jonathan, which is good with an animal like that. Not bad at all. Now let's hope Thea can pull out a good round—'

And seeing Thea, very wiry and competent-looking, waiting at the start, Ruth realized that, herself apart, Mrs. Meredith's team was in fact a very experienced team, and it was no great surprise that they were doing so well. She was the only weak link. If it had been her waiting to go now, instead of Thea, none of them would have looked nearly so optimistic. As it was, their optimism was fully justified, and they won second place and only missed the challenge cup by two points. Ruth, on the edge of this triumph, now fully recovered, but feeling oddly insulated from the general elation, rode home in the back of the lorry wondering if her chance would ever come to make good. Her modest ambition was a distant star, clouded almost beyond perception. She did not feel all there, and cried when she was in bed—but quietly, so that Ted would not hear.

15

R UTH felt that her fate was irrevocably sealed when Mrs. Meredith informed her that she was definitely entered in the Area Trials team on Toad, thanks to Toad's excellent showing at Pickworth.

'Peter's excellent showing,' Ruth said, but Mrs. Meredith gave her a bland smile and said, 'But of course you can do it too! Especially after a week at camp. You'll find you'll really be working together well. I have complete confidence in you.'

Ruth thought that the woman was a good liar, but said no more. Mere silence could, if she were lucky, be misconstrued as quiet confidence.

'The Trials take place the day before camp finishes, so it will really be very convenient. We can box up and get away early, all being on the spot. And the ponies should really be going well by then.'

Ruth found that she was, in fact, looking forward to camp. Having Thea to share with made a difference. Mrs. Parker drove their trailer over the day before camp started, and left it in the marked-out field, where the living accommodation was to be pitched. The girls' quarters were lined up down one hedge, and the boys' down the opposite one: the plushy Meredith caravan was already in place, but Jonathan had the least plushy job of all when the girls arrived, digging the latrines. His father was there, organizing the erecting of the large marquees which served as dining-hall and kitchen; he was a large cheerful man, very handy with a mallet, and—in a tattered jersey full of holes and sailcloth trousers —not looking much like the city tycoon he was reputed to be. The field was aswarm with helpers, and Ruth and Thea, having put their trailer in line, filled with lilos, sleeping-bags, buckets and gum-boots, were soon roped in to help unload cooking gear from crates in the kitchen. The familiar smell of the draughty tent, of treated canvas and tarred ropes and calor gas and crushed, damp grass, made Ruth feel immediately at home. She had been to two camps before, with Fly-by-Night—it was only the thought of Fly-by-Night now, remembering his cocky eagerness over the Maybridge grass, his exuberant bucks when he came out for inspection in the morning, and his madcap galloping over the cross-country course which had first caused Mrs. Meredith to notice her, that gave Ruth pause for reflection, provoking the miserable pangs that afflicted her whenever she thought of his condition. Last year he had been her pride and joy. She felt that she had let him down cruelly, and the camp-site reminded her now, bitterly. She worked hard to take her mind off it, and was rewarded for her energy by being upgraded to latrine-digging with Jonathan, Mr. Meredith finding another spade in somebody's Landrover. While she dug, she told Jonathan about having seen Fly-by-Night again, but Jonathan said, 'If he's not actually for sale, I don't see how you can do anything about it.'

'Even if he is, I can't. I haven't any money.'

Jonathan wasn't in a very good mood, latrine-digging not being his favourite job.

'McNair's your best bet. He knows he's a good pony. But you can't do much unless he's advertised.' He straightened up, and wiped the sweat off his face with his jersey arm. 'Talking of McNairs, have you seen Sirius?'

'What, here, you mean?'

'Yes, in the bottom meadow. He looks really good—fit, I mean. It seems a pity Peter can't use him for camp.'

Ruth hesitated. Then she said, 'Peter's been riding him. He comes down here out of school.'

Jonathan grinned. 'I guessed it. There's a ridden track in the field, worn bare, and the pony looks really good.'

'Don't say anything. Thea and I both know—she saw him. He plays truant. Nobody seems to have found out yet.'

'He's crazy! What if his father finds out?'

'Don't say anything, for Heaven's sake!'

'No, as if I would! But if his father ever sets eyes on him—Sirius, I mean. He's as fit as a fiddle. No fat on him at all. He'd know.'

'Well, Peter must know what he's doing.'

Peter arrived at camp with Solomon's Seal the following morning, and installed him in one of the loose boxes that the more privileged members were accorded, instead of a cowstall in the barn where most of the ponies were stabled. (Mr. McNair always insisted on his rights.) He then repaired to Jonathan's caravan for coffee, and Thea and Ruth, fresh from the trials of changing out of jeans and into jodhpurs in the confines of the Parker pony-trailer full of beds and suitcases, joined them to admire the pure luxury of high-class camping. Jonathan showed them all the ingenious gadgets, happy to exploit male superiority. Jessica, apparently, had to make do with the Meredith's 'old' caravan, and Mrs. Meredith was sharing Mrs. Towler's.

'How come you got the best?' Thea asked.

'I said I wouldn't come if I didn't. Mother was buttering me up. I asked when she was in a good mood.'

When it rained, Ruth and Thea had to move their beds according to the leaks, and borrow a New Zealand rug for the worst bits from Mr. Harper, the Maybridge farmer. Jonathan and Peter merely shut the window, turned over and went to sleep again. It rained a lot. The weather was very warm, humid, and the rain was warm, drifting across the heavy fields and running in the ditches. In the evenings, when everyone else had repaired early with cups of cocoa and comics and Dick Francis thrillers, Peter went down to the bottom meadow and rode Sirius. Ruth and Thea, wanting comfort, went across to Jonathan, and lay on his soft bunks to read and talk. They all knew where Peter was.

'Does your mother know?' Thea asked Jonathan.

'If she does, I don't think she'll bother,' Jonathan said. 'Not her pigeon.'

He was lying on his back, twiddling with the transistor. He didn't play the usual Radio One, but Mozart on the Third. Ruth had never come across anyone quite like Jonathan before. She was supposed to be reading, but watched him from behind the useful curtain of her hair, brushed out loose ready for bed.

'I don't know how he can be bothered,' he said.

They were all tired in the evening, after riding all day, and doing evening stables and all the chores, carrying water, washing up, tack-cleaning. Ruth enjoyed physical weariness: it was always connected with horses in her experience, and she was acutely aware of the pleasure of resting, curled up, listening to the music and the soft whispering of the rain on the roof, watching Jonathan. All the time she was conscious of the big competition at the end of the week. Each day was one day nearer, and each day she felt she had to think about it, look at the prospect squarely, and not be afraid. It was really going to happen this time, her testing, and there would be no substitutes, no excuses. To the others it wasn't anything much at all, but to her it was a great landmark, like a lighthouse in her path, all her energies to be gathered to it. She wished she didn't have to take things so seriously, but she couldn't help it.

'It'll be hefty going on Friday, if this weather keeps up,' Jonathan remarked.

'It doesn't look as if it's ever going to stop,' Thea said. The clouds seemed to be touching the ground. The next day they had to give up their jumping session with Gary Major, when the rain set in hard in the middle of the afternoon. The jumps, set up in the flattest field on the far side of the farm, were high and severe, and Ruth had wanted to try them, her final test before Friday. But they had to put the ponies away and repair to the big marquee for early tea, and had a lecture instead, on first aid and common diseases of the horse. Jonathan read 'Sailing Alone Around the World' all the way through it. After tea it cleared enough for a barbecue supper, and after all the juniors had been stuffed full of burnt sausages, the seniors had to form a working party to get duck-boards down at the doors of the tents and caravans and on the traffic ways to the various communal tents. Peter had no time to ride Sirius, Ruth remarked. He was in the caravan at cocoa-time, but nobody remarked on his activities.

That night it rained again. Ruth lay listening to it, remembering Jonathan's words. It was still very warm. Very English, she thought. She could smell the wet earth and the hawthorn hedges, pungent, and hear the water trickling through the ditch nearby. There was something else too, the thud of hooves on the far side of the hedge. Soft and splashy, but unmistakeable. Very regular, a ridden horse, not a loose one. Or was it a loose one? She ought to get up and have a look. She lay still. Behind the clouds there was a full moon; the square of sky at the back of the trailer was luminous, and in spite of the rain the night was bright. If there was a horse there, she would be able to see it.

Thea was sleeping heavily and did not wake up when Ruth stepped over her. She reached for her anorak and put it on, and opened the door, groping with a bare foot for the gum-boots kicked underneath out of the wet. The big camping field lay brightly, gleaming and shining, trembling with rain. Nothing moved. She shut the door behind her and started to walk across to the gate, to look into the next field. Wide awake now, the dampness infiltrating, she thought she was being a bit stupid.

She got to the gate and looked across the next field, but could see nothing. She leaned on the gate, thinking about Friday, and heard the sound of hooves again. They were far away, beyond the field she was looking into, beyond the big barns where the ponies were stabled. In the jumping field, in fact. She looked up sharply. Then she climbed over the gate and started to hurry across the intervening field, scraping her bare heels in the boots, the warm rain lying like a web over her hair.

She knew before she got there what she was going to see. She

could see in her mind what was happening, matched to the now quite definite thudding of hooves on the grass. Peter was crazy, there was no doubt about it, but Ruth, running now, excited, was glad that there were other crazy people besides herself. And splendid crazy, not just stupid crazy like her. It was mad to jump those jumps in the dark and the rain, but Peter had Sirius beautifully in hand, completely under control, more calm than Ruth had ever seen him or imagined he could be. The jumps were all set at their highest, using all the poles, and Sirius, when Ruth got to the bottom gate, was just turning to go into the triple-bar, the biggest of them all. But this time there was no panic at all; it was copybook jumping, steadying up for the turn—Ruth could see Peter standing up, his hands holding, so that Sirius was almost at a standstill, yet still cantering, winding up like a spring, then Peter sat down firmly and Sirius uncoiled, his long stride reaching out, the enormous power in his hocks lifting him over the big jump as if it were just a single pole on a few bricks. And afterwards he pulled up without even a shake of his head. Peter leaned forward and patted him and said something to him, and then turned and came back towards the gate, letting all the reins out. He was smiling to himself; Ruth could see, almost feel, his content.

She opened the gate for him. He pulled up and looked down at her. He was wearing his pyjamas and plimsolls and a jersey covered in mud and a red bobble hat pulled down over his ears.

'He was marvellous,' Ruth said.

'Yes. I said he could.'

Peter rode through, and Ruth shut the gate behind him.

'I wasn't spying,' she said. 'I was awake and I heard the hooves and I thought I'd better see, in case it was a pony got out. But then I realised, and I came to watch anyway.'

'It doesn't matter,' Peter said. 'As long as no one else sees. I'll go back the other side of the barns, not through camp.'

Ruth slipped in the mud and nearly fell flat on her face. Peter pulled up and took his foot out of the stirrup.

'Come up too.' He reached down and helped her up, sliding farther back in the saddle to make room. It seemed to Ruth suddenly very warm and friendly to be sitting there, and so many things to be happy about, Sirius plodding on like an old nag.

'We knew you were riding him,' she said.

'Well, it doesn't matter. As long as my father doesn't know. Not yet, at least. He's by far the best nag I've ever ridden. That triple was over five feet and nearly five foot spread. He did it three times, and

each time with some to spare. I've never had jumps, you see, until
they moved the camp ones in, so I thought I'd make the most of the

opportunity. Hope old mother Meredith didn't hear anything.'

'I doubt it.'

They squelched back under the shadow of the big weather-boarded barns, through banks of cow-parsley and a gap in the hedge, over a ditch and up through a ride of hazel trees. They had to bend low, the wet leaves drenching them. Ruth felt Peter's arms round her, warm and secure, and although they were there to hold the reins, she also sensed that Peter was liking it too. And, as if in confirmation, he put his head down close for a moment and said, 'We ought to do this more often.' It was his old voice, funny and mocking. Ruth felt that she could scarcely remember him like this, it had been so long since he had been friendly.

'Except that I have a nasty feeling you've got your beady little eye on Jonathan,' he added. 'I've noticed signs.'

'Have you?' Ruth was surprised.

'You admit it?'

'I admit nothing.'

'Hmm. I draw my own conclusions. I thought it was only the ponies that were competing.'

They got back to Sirius's field and untacked him. Peter dried off the saddle as best he could with the front of his jersey, washed the bits and the muddy stirrup irons in the wet grass, and hung it all up tidily in the barn. He rubbed Sirius down with a hay-wisp and turned him loose. The pony nuzzled at him briefly, then walked away down the field, his nose in the grass. He was perfectly undisturbed. They watched him go, both content to admire him. He looked as fit as Railway, the muscle hard and rippling over his back and quarters.

'Does he only get grass?' Ruth asked. 'He looks magnificent.'

'He gets oats as well, which I steal,' Peter said. 'Say no more. Mr. Harper's seen me, actually, caught me red-handed, but he didn't mind. He's well-disposed, which is useful, as I'm hoping he'll cope with my daddy when the day comes.'

'What day?'

'The day when all is known. Our sins are revealed. We stand before our Maker and all that.'

'Oh, yes, I see. Poor you.' Mr. McNair was all right as long as everyone was doing what he wanted. Peter had a cross to bear in that direction. But perhaps that was a general tendency among parents. Ruth hadn't come up against it yet. She rather thought

Jonathan had, judging by the flinty confrontations she had witnessed at times.

They started back to camp, moving cautiously. It was still raining and Ruth's hair was beginning to drip down her neck unpleasantly, and she could feel the dampness coming through her jacket and across her shoulders. Peter was soaked through.

'Couldn't be any wetter,' he said cheerfully. 'You look a bit of a drip too. Come back to Meredith Manor and get dried out—hot coffee and all that. We might as well make the most of our privileges.'

Ruth was grateful. The thought of her cold lilo in the leaking trailer was not inviting. They crept cautiously back through the camp and let themselves into the Meredith caravan. Peter put the light on and pulled all the curtains to and put the kettle on. Jonathan groaned and opened his eyes, screwing his face up against the light.

'Cripes, what are you up to?'

'A nice cup of tea,' Peter said soothingly. 'You too, my sleeping beauty. What do you think of his pyjamas, Ruth? Just for camping in too, not his best ones.'

They were crimson and black silk stripes, with black lapels with red piping round, and a black sash, very beautiful.

Jonathan grinned. 'You're jealous. God, what do you think you look like? Is that your midnight riding gear? Or am I giving away secrets?' He glanced at Ruth, worried for a moment.

'No. She thought I was a loose horse and came to catch me. She knows all.'

'What, everything? About—'

'No, for God's sake. Shut up. Not about that.'

Jonathan rubbed his eyes wearily. He looked gloomy suddenly. 'I wish it was all over. Especially Friday. Get on with that tea, you louse. I was happy, unconscious. You ruin every damned thing.'

Peter was stripping off in the kitchen, and came back trailing a Meredith bath-towel, with monogram, tied round his waist, and the wet red bobble hat from which his hair stood out in spikes all round. Ruth, feeling very tired all of a sudden, took off her anorak and sat down on the spare bunk. Peter made the tea and brought the teapot in and put it on the floor. A dog barked from the top of the field, and Jonathan paused, tea-cup in mid-air.

'That's Paddy.' Paddy was Mrs. Meredith's dog and slept under the caravan. 'Anyone on the prowl?'

Peter looked cautiously out of the window. 'A torch, coming this way.'

'Oh, blast. I suppose we're lit up like a lighthouse from outside.' Discipline was strict about larks in the night. 'For Heaven's sake—'

There was a mad scramble. 'Ruth—in the kitchen! No, she'll look in there—'

'The wardrobe!'

'Put her jacket under the bunk.'

'All these flaming wellies—'

They shut Ruth in the wardrobe, bent double and unable to breathe and kicked her third tea cup under Peter's wet pyjamas just as Mrs. Meredith put her head round the door. Ruth, frozen into her crouched position in the stuffy dark, pictured Peter standing there in his weird get-up, trying to look as if he normally made tea dressed in a bath-towel and a bobble hat in the middle of the night.

'What on earth— ?' Mrs. Meredith sounded at her worst, tired and dragonish. 'I've just been coping with Malcolm Morrison, who's made himself sick with a midnight feast of liquorice allsorts and beer, and I saw your light on—really, it's too bad, you seniors! Peter, why are you—are these your pyjamas, all wet? What on earth are you up to? Where've you been?'

'I had to—er—go down to the—er—and it was raining—'

'You must have been down there all night by the look of you. Are you all right?'

Ruth heard Jonathan say, 'No, he's been out there for ages. You can see. I said why don't you use the one in here, and he said—'

'Oh, Peter—you've got this tummy-bug, I suppose? You have been looking a bit under the weather, I noticed tonight—as if you've not been getting your sleep. I've got some stuff that'll put you right. It's not very nice to take, but very good. I'll go and fetch it.'

'Honestly, I'm not—it's all right now—'

Ruth, holding her breath, found it was now emerging in uncontrollable hiccups of giggles. She heard Jonathan give a snort, and turn it into an urgent cough.

'There must be no fear of your not being quite right for Friday. Get back into bed now, and I'll go and get this stuff. You must keep warm. Have you got another pair of pyjamas? No? Jonathan has—get them out, Jonathan, and give them to Peter. I'll be back in a minute.'

She retreated and Peter leapt on Jonathan and knocked him to the floor. Jonathan was choking with laughter, and Ruth rattled on the door, shrieking to be let out, listening to the thumps and crashings and Peter's dire and blasphemous opinions as to Jonathan's character. The caravan rocked.

'For a sick man you're—' Jonathan's voice was strangled suddenly.

Ruth, suffocating, burst open the door by straightening up hard, and shot out into the light into the tangle of bodies.

'You fools!' she hissed. 'Buck up—'

She glanced out of the door. 'She's coming back, for Heaven's sake. If you'd let me out I'd have had time to go. Shut me back in, quick! For Heaven's sake—'

The boys got up and shot round straightening everything, slamming the door shut on Ruth again. Ruth could feel herself bursting again, half-hysterical, as Mrs. Meredith spooned her awful mixture down Peter's throat and waited for him to get back into bed. When she had put the light out and departed Peter lay there groaning and clutching his stomach. Jonathan let Ruth out.

'She's more used to drenching horses, you can tell,' Peter complained. 'What a mother! I wonder she didn't use a twitch. You deserve everything you get, Meredith. I—'

'Hark who's talking!' Jonathan said. 'When I think what *I'm* conniving at for your sake—'

'*Shut up!*' Peter roared. 'God Almighty, is nothing sacred? I'm going to be sick.'

'Well, mind my pyjamas. They're my best ones. I'm going back to sleep.'

Ruth decided to make her escape before anything else happened. She groped for her anorak and gum-boots and let herself out. The boys were complete idiots, but Peter's unbending was the nicest thing that had happened for a long time. Of course, he had been in a good mood, after Sirius had performed so well. It might be different again tomorrow. Ruth felt happy and tired. There was something else that needed thinking about, the hints that had been dropped concerning some secret which she didn't know about, something the two of them were plotting between themselves, but by the time she was back in bed again she was too tired to bother.

She slept heavily, and did not wake up again till Thea trod on her in the morning.

16

RUTH found the day very long, keyed up with nerves for the Trials the day after. The four of them were dropped out of the afternoon activities, to rest their ponies, and were supposed to spend the time making sure their tack and clothes were in order and then helping Mrs. Towler and Mr. Major to plan the various competitions for the last day of camp. Ruth found that her own competition so preoccupied her mind that she was not of much use to anybody, but strangely enough, the two boys seemed similarly afflicted.

'If I didn't know you better, I would have said you were suffering from nerves,' Mrs. Towler said severely to Jonathan, after he had copied the wrong list of competitors on to her carefully prepared scoring sheet. 'You're all of you at half-cock as far as the required mental application is concerned. I think you'd be better off resting.'

'A kindly way of telling us she'd get on better without us,' as Thea pointed out, having departed. 'I must say Peter and Jonathan are acting in a very strange manner.'

Ruth hadn't noticed.

'What do you mean?'

'Shifty-looking.'

Ruth remembered her suspicions of the night before, that the boys were plotting something, but now it didn't seem very important compared with her own troubles. Thea found her poor company, and they went to bed early. It rained. Ruth felt that she lay awake all night listening to it, hoping that perhaps if it rained enough the event would be cancelled. She could hear it running in the ditch under the hedge, dropping from the hawthorn in heavy, irregular drops long after it had stopped drumming on the trailer roof. In the morning, with the light, the sky was deep grey with greenish-yellow streaks of dawn. They had to get up very early. Frozen and shivering, Ruth washed in the cold ablutions tent, the canvas flapping sullenly around her, the mud squishing up between the slats of the slimy duckboards. The cold water penetrated right to the heart; she wanted to die. She went out to the stables and fed Toad. It was warmer out there, the surprised, sleepy ponies giving off a communal fug under the low barn roofs, which leaked a lot less than the trailer. She saw Peter, yawning, carrying a bucket of oats away out of the yard—to Sirius, she supposed—but he didn't say anything. Jonathan, measuring out a large scoopful of horsenuts, was equally uncommunicative, and did not even smile.

One of the cooks had got them an early breakfast, and they ate it at one of the long tables in the mess tent. Mrs. Meredith came out to them in a camel-hair dressing-gown with a mac thrown over it and gum-boots and said, 'You can get groomed and boxed up on your own, can't you? I'll be in the yard about a quarter to eight. Sally is going to put some food up for us so don't forget to come and collect it. Pity about the weather. Sorry I can't help now, but the rest of the camp has to proceed as usual and there's obviously going to be a lot of drying out to cope with . . .'

Her spirit in adversity was admirable, Ruth could not help remarking, glancing out at the sodden field and the life stirring out of the tents and caravans. However hard it might rain, the ponies still had to be cared for and ridden out, and all the little mother's darlings dried off, fed and suitably amused whatever the difficulties.

'At least it seems to rain mostly at night-times. I suppose we should be thankful for that.'

She looked at them doubtfully, picking at their bacon and baked beans in the cold, saggy cavern of the waterlogged tent, and departed without another word. Ruth noticed Peter and Jonathan exchange meaningful glances, but what they were up to she had no idea, nor the will to wonder.

She went back to the stable and applied herself to the business of making Toad as beautiful as possible. This did not take very long, so polished had he been all the week, his mane and tail already washed. She bandaged his legs and tail and put a sheet over him and went to see how the others were getting on. It was half-past seven. Jonathan had finished Railway and was gathering up his grooming tools. He was looking at his watch.

'Thea and I are ready,' Ruth said. 'Where's Peter?'

'We'll box up if you two go and get the food and the gear,' Jonathan said. 'We haven't a lot of time.'

Ruth thought they'd been doing pretty well. The box was standing in the middle of the yard ready, the ramp down.

'Peter and I have left our things out on the bunks—can you collect them? Ma'll be here on the dot. I'll put Toad in.'

'Okay.' Ruth would rather have put Toad in herself, but didn't want to argue.

Peter appeared from the far side of the yard and came over to the box. 'Tell Thea Sally wants her. The food or something.'

'All right.'

They were being unusually managing, it struck Ruth, but everything seemed well in hand, with none of the more common last-minute rush. She collected Thea and told her the boys were boxing the ponies, and that she had to go and collect the food.

'Oh, do I? Why me?'

'Peter said.'

'Huh.'

Thea trailed away across the field and Ruth went into the boys' caravan and collected up their kit which was laid out in uncommonly immaculate order on the bunks. She put the two riding caps on her head, and one crash-helmet, and gathered up the coats and jerseys, but couldn't manage the two pairs of gleaming boots and the other crash-helmet as well, so set out with what she could manage. Jonathan met her at the entrance to the yard and took it all off her and she went back for the second load. Thea appeared and said, 'Peter's up the wall. Sally's already given the food to Mrs. M. Why are they being so bossy? Why can't they collect their own gear?'

'I don't know.'

'We've still got to get ours.'

Ruth took her second armful. The ponies were apparently all loaded, for Peter was putting up the ramp and Jonathan was squashing everything up in the groom's department to make room. Ruth handed her things up to him.

'We'll put your tack in,' Jonathan said.

Ruth went for her own things, and arrived back at the lorry just as Mrs. Meredith appeared, pulling on her driving gloves. Mr. Milburn, the old goat, was coming with her, and nobody wanted to share the driving-cab with him, all electing to go in the back.

Mrs. Meredith eyed Ruth fiercely and said, 'You won't be sick this time?'

'No. Honestly.'

'You're sure you've all got everything? All your tack? Studs if you want them? Hats?'

'Yes, we've checked.'

'In you get then. We're right on the dot.'

They scrambled in and she slammed the door on them. The throaty diesel engine rumbled into life, and one of the ponies whinnied nervously.

Jonathan leaned his head back against the partition and said, 'Thank God that's over.'

'What on earth do you mean? We haven't started yet,' Thea said.

Jonathan didn't reply. Ruth looked at him curiously, then at Peter. Peter, in the gloom, looked as white as a sheet.

'I don't know about me feeling sick,' she said. 'You look as if you're going to spew up at any moment.'

Peter made a face, and said, 'I'm all right.' But he sounded very edgy. In the turmoil of getting started, Ruth had stopped being nervous, but seeing Peter, obviously screwed up, her stomach gave a fresh turn in sympathy. If *he* was nervous . . .

'What's wrong with you?' she asked.

'Nothing.'

'Nothing that isn't apparent if you use your eyes,' Jonathan said. 'You might as well tell them now. We've done the tricky bit.'

'You have,' Peter said. 'Speak for yourself. I haven't even started yet.'

'Well, that's your pigeon. It's what you wanted, isn't it? And if you hash it up, it's me that's got to live with the D.C., who'll rave for days—'

'Oh, shut up,' Peter said.

'So nice to have two raving idiots for travelling companions,' Thea said amiably to Ruth. 'It fills me with confidence to be part of such a half-baked team.'

Ruth supposed that if she hadn't been so tied up with her own feelings of apprehension she would have guessed what was going on much sooner. But as it was she had given the boys' odd behaviour very little thought. Now, as soon as she did, the reason for it was quite apparent. She stood up and peered over into the horse-

quarters, Toad was the inside pony, and beyond him, the white
stripe on his face shining as he peered back at her over his partition,
was—

'Sirius!'

She looked down at Peter, filled with admiration.

'What a marvellous idea! Whyever didn't you say? It's fantastic!'

'I'm glad somebody thinks so,' Peter said.

'You mean he's got Sirius in there instead of Solomon?' Thea
demanded. 'Holy Cow, what's the D.C. going to say?'

'She doesn't know?' Ruth's admiration turned to stunned awe.
'Not yet.'

'God Almighty! What's she going to say?'

'An interesting point,' Jonathan said. 'We're rather wondering
ourselves.' His voice remarkably lacked confidence.

'We can't wait to hear,' Peter agreed.

'We're agog in fact.'

Ruth sat back to digest the situation. She found it distinctly
alarming, although she wasn't directly involved. Jonathan would
get a blasting for aiding and abetting, but Peter . . . Peter had
taken a gamble of the most enormous proportions.

'You'll have to do well,' she said inadequately, 'else—'

'Oh, Christ, you don't have to tell me,' he muttered.

'Individual champion, no less,' Jonathan said.

'Is your father coming?' Ruth asked.

'I hope not. But I don't know.'

'If he is, he might stop you riding.'

'I'm counting on Mrs. M. being a match for him. She'll be
furious, but she wouldn't let him break up her team at the last
minute, I'm sure.'

Ruth, who for so long had wished that her parents were horsy
and took an intelligent interest, now vowed that she would never
again do anything but bless their lovely ignorance. Peter and
Jonathan both had to justify their actions to their respective parents
before anything else, and it was only because of this that what
might normally be quite a lark was now taking on such grave proportions. Peter was in fact challenging the formidable adult judgement, and was quite possibly—if anything went wrong—forfeiting
Sirius's life by what he had chosen to do. That he realized this was
quite plain. Left to himself, he would have taken Sirius confidently

137

and cheerfully. Ruth, silent now, wondered what drove some parents to make all this business matter so desperately, when it was supposed to be nothing but an enjoyable sport. That it mattered to her, personally, was her own business and quite in order, but that one was driven to excellence out of self-defence, bowing to superior forces, seemed quite absurd. Her own mother would be getting breakfast now, probably not even aware that today was her daughter's making or breaking day—turning Ted's fried egg over on the other side the way he liked it and trying to read the local paper at the same time before Ted came down and bagged it. If her mother was worried, it would be for the dampness of the weather, and nothing to do with prowess on horseback. Ruth sent her a silent prayer of gratitude for being what she was and resolved never to criticise her again. She also felt urgent pangs of sympathy for Peter in his lonely predicament which made her own nervousness seem perfectly ridiculous by comparison, but there was little any of them could do to help. Their joint sympathy was fairly evident, laced with the communal fascinated curiosity as to Mrs. Meredith's reaction when she found out. The journey passed in glum apprehension, the edginess increasing as the miles spun out. Peter was completely silent, sunk into the collar of his polo-necked jersey, his hands clasped round his knees.

Eventually the horse-box came off the road and started bumping slowly over the grass. Ruth got up and looked out of the window and saw acres of rain-flattened pasture, very hilly, divided by big natural hedges, with a ridge of woodland running over the horizon, no doubt to be closely explored in the course of the cross-country. The box went down into a valley and through a gateway and up the side of the next hill to where the horse-lines were marked out, and large marquees, strongly tethered, breathed heavily in the cold, unsummer-like wind. A copse, wired round, sheltered the parking area. Mrs. Meredith parked with the ramp to the trees. When the engine cut out, the silence was charged with incipient doom. Ruth caught Jonathan's eye, and grimaced, but not very jokily. It was going to be no joke.

They piled out shivering as the grey morning swept in on their fug. Bright Morning was kicking away inside—one of his more tiresome habits—and Mrs. Meredith said, 'You might as well unload first. It's nice and sheltered here and you've brought rugs, haven't you? I don't want my new box broken up.' She looked in an unusually good humour and beamed cheerfully upon them all. 'My word, you all look very serious! I don't think it will be as bad as you think.'

They all knew it would, but the boys let the ramp down obediently and Jonathan brought out Railway. Thea went in for Bright Morning and Peter waited, staring at his gum-boots. Jonathan tied Railway up and came back and stood by his mother, which Ruth thought was noble, and Thea led Bright Morning down the ramp. Peter disappeared inside the box, in no hurry. Mrs. Meredith was chatting to Mr. Milburn about her point-to-point year with Florestan and was in the middle of saying, 'This gelding of Peter's started in point-to-points,' when Peter led Sirius down the ramp. Mr. Milburn looked at him and said, 'A bit small for that game, surely?'

Mrs. Meredith frowned. Peter, not looking at her, led Sirius clear of the ramp and walked him round to the far side of the box to tie him up.

Mrs. Meredith looked at Jonathan. Ruth, seeing her expression, almost ran up the ramp into the blessed recess of the lorry to where Toad was waiting, darling and familiar. She untied him, burying her face in his lovely smelly mane and saying, 'Oh, preserve us! God save us!' She wanted to stay where she was, but realized that solid support was urgently required outside. She almost ran with Toad down the ramp and lined herself up close by Peter, who was saying doggedly, 'He's better than Solomon by miles.'

Mrs. Meredith was livid, her face tightened up in a strange and unfamiliar way, her aristocratic nostrils extended like her own horse's after a race. Ruth looked at her, almost hypnotized. No wonder Jonathan stepped with care!

'The deceit of it! Not even asking, discussing the matter, but quite unscrupulously putting your own personal desire before any thought for the good of the team . . . utter, cold-blooded disobedience! If you really think you can get away with this sort of behaviour, Peter, you must underestimate me—expecting me to be blackmailed into presenting an unfit, dangerous rogue of the first order to represent our team just because you prefer your own judgement—'

'He's as fit as Railway. I've been riding him every day for the last two months.'

'You have been forbidden to go near him!'

'Yes, well—'

'Does your father know?'

'No.'

'Is your father coming today?'

'I hope not.'

Ruth thought Mrs. Meredith was going to explode. Her nostrils closed in tightly, the ridge of her nose seeming to stand out more sharply, like a mountain crag. She seemed aware herself of the danger of losing control, for she said, very carefully, 'Peter, go away. Out of my sight. I need a drink.'

She went round to the cab of the horse-box. Mr. Milburn,

looking more than ever like an old goat, but a very cross one, said, 'Really, Peter, this isn't team behaviour, you know. You have put Mrs. Meredith in an impossible situation. I'm very surprised at you, with your experience.'

Jonathan followed his mother, who was sitting in the cab with a whisky-flask in her hand. Ruth had to tie Toad up at the cab end, where she was sitting, as the others had taken the other places, so she overheard Jonathan's approach.

'Mother, it's not as bad as you think. Peter does know what he's doing. Sirius is going superbly, he's been working on him all the time—you know what he's like—'

'Jonathan, don't make it worse! Do you think I don't know the facts? I'm not stupid. But you are stupid, both of you, not to have had this out with me earlier, instead of springing it on me in this impossible manner. What am I to answer to Mr. McNair, if Peter has an accident? Even if he doesn't, the position is quite untenable. The man might well turn up today, and in any case will know all about it by tonight, the grapevine being what it is. I don't think you have any idea of—' Her voice rose in fresh fury, and she stopped herself, and took another mouthful of whisky. It struck Ruth that she was very well-schooled, like her own Florestan.

'And you—to have let it happen! I despair of you sometimes, that you can be so foolish! Your father will have to deal with this, just as no doubt Mr. McNair will sort Peter out.'

'But meanwhile,' Jonathan said stubbornly, 'if Peter rides, you've got a first-class team. Much better than if he had been on Solomon, who doesn't like soft going. You *know* this. And it's the team that matters—you've said so all along. The best at any price.'

'Will you go away, Jonathan! You are not helping. I know my position very well—particularly my misfortune in having such a pair of imbeciles in my charge. I must talk to Jack. We are in a very difficult situation and I might well have to withdraw. Jack!'

'You can't withdraw!' Jonathan said, horrified.

'Go away,' said his mother.

Mr. Milburn came round to the cab and Mrs. Meredith offered him the whisky bottle. Ruth thought if they drank enough everything would probably come all right. She, like Jonathan, was a bit appalled at the idea of having to withdraw.

'I say, we can't withdraw,' Jonathan said to her. They went round to Peter who was sitting on the ramp with his head in his hands. 'She's talking about withdrawing.'

'You mustn't let her!' Peter said. 'That's absolutely crazy! We've got a good chance of winning—better than if it had been Solomon. She only thinks about winning, doesn't she? I mean, I've done her a favour, if she did but know it.'

'She's frightened of your daddy, if you get killed.'

'Solomon'd kill me. He goes through everything. He doesn't know how hard they nail them on round here. You tell her my daddy didn't do what he was told when he was little, either. I've heard him brag about it. He's no room to talk at all. Besides which, we're going to do so well that his knacker's nag will be worth four figures by the end of the day.'

'Individual champion?'

'Well, why not?' Peter muttered.

Mrs. Meredith was climbing out of the cab. She came back and considered Peter, then turned to Mr. Milburn. 'Jack, get the boy a nip of whisky. He looks terrible. We've decided not to stand in your way, Peter, if you want to break your neck. My team's more important. But, my God, if you don't pull all the stops out and show us you were right—' She shrugged, and the beginnings of a smile showed, which she checked before it got through. Mr. Milburn handed Peter the whisky flask. 'I'll go and sort out the substitution—I'll have to spin a tale, I suppose, but I dare say they'll accept it. Off you go and have a look at the course-map, then we'll walk round and look at it together. The going will be very treacherous, I don't need to tell you.'

The pall of gloom lifted instantly. Ruth felt all her own nervousness race back, her stomach apparently turning over of its own accord; glanced at Peter, saw his grim face, and reminded herself that, if there was any worrying to be done, it was mainly in Peter's department. Today was her great chance to show that she was not, in fact, an imbecile. She thought of Ted, and made herself look cool and smiling. Jonathan and Thea were highly delighted, and they walked up to the Secretary's tent looking like a quite normal, sane, well-brought-up Pony Club team. While Mrs. Meredith spun her tale about Solomon turning out lame and there not being any time to get a vet's certificate, they studied the course-map pinned up on the side of a horse-trailer. Ruth left it to the others to prophesy the worst of the hazards; she would wait until she saw them in the flesh. The coloured inks, arrows and dotted lines could not in her mind be linked with the vast grey, cloud-swept landscape that surrounded her. She stood with her parka hood pulled up, staring down the hill towards the start, and wondering how she would be feeling some six hours or so later. She kept thinking of Ted, almost desperately. She wished he was there, more than anybody.

Mrs. Meredith emerged from the Secretary's trailer, holding their numbers.

'It's all right. All set to go. Our first dressage is at eleven twenty, so we've plenty of time. You've looked at the map? Very well, let's go.'

It started off innocuously enough, over some straw-bales, away from the tents and over a ditch and rail into the next field. Already the first ditch was swollen with water, presenting a more formidable obstacle than was probably originally intended, and was quite difficult to negotiate on foot. The rail was wired on, and definitely not to be hit. The next obstacle stood alone in the middle of the field beyond, and was an in-and-out of telegraph poles, with the out bit having to be jumped at right angles to the in, which meant being thoroughly under control. Sacks of peat were piled nearby, which were no doubt anticipating the nasty muddy mess the middle of the jump would quickly become.

'It's too small,' Jonathan said. 'Railway'll land on the far side.'

'Only if you let him,' his mother said.

The course turned back towards the start and through a gateway, immediately left-handed along the hedge and then down an awkward bank, preceded by a fixed bar, into a sunken lane and left-handed back towards the far hillside again. Crossed poles clear in the middle of the ensuing gallop were straightforward. They glanced at them and plodded on, the water squelching out underfoot. The field sloped up gradually to one of the wide belts of woodland and the course entered it over an imposing fixed bank of railway sleepers, solid as a house, crossed the corner through cleared shrub and went out over a very big ditch, brimming and gurgling in a series of swollen waterfalls towards lower ground and the main stream in the valley. There had been a fixed rail on the far side of this obstacle as well, but two stewards were in the act of dismantling it.

'Nasty enough without,' one of them said to Mrs. Meredith. 'The conditions are dictating a few changes, I'm afraid.'

The drop to this ditch was very soft and peaty, making a bad take-off. The four of them stood considering it, not very happily. It made Ruth feel queasy, looking at it. She said to Peter, 'What will Toad do here?'

'Leave it to him. He'll probably wade through. Hold on to his mane and just push him on, lots of rein. Pray.'

She thought she would have exhausted her stock of prayers by this stage. They crossed the ditch by means of a plank thoughtfully placed on one side for the purpose, and came out into open field again. Ruth was not feeling very happy, but noticed that the others were looking serious too; she didn't have to pretend anything.

The course, having emerged, appeared to change its mind almost immediately, for it went back into the woods some thirty

144

yards down, this time over a solid bridge of sleepers and through a gate, pinned open. The ride through the woods was cramped and twisting with three obstacles before it emerged: a very large fallen tree, some rails nailed solidly between two oaks and a big pile of faggots and brush. The problem here would be to jump them almost the moment one saw them, and not have the pony making amazed refusals at the suddenness of their appearance. It meant quick decisions, and being very well in hand, and not getting a faceful of wet leaves at the wrong moment. Ruth was not encouraged. They continued along the track, and came out into the top field again by means of a sharp scramble up a rooty bank and an awkward jump out over a pile of brush with a knock-down rail on top.

'Very difficult not to knock down,' Mrs. Meredith pronounced. 'Nasty trick.'

'It's all a bit nasty,' Jonathan said. 'Especially if we don't go until fairly late on. Do we?'

'No, I'm afraid not. About three-quarters of the way through.'

'It'll all be nicely mashed up by then,' Peter said. 'Our poor little quads will be sucked under.'

It had started to rain again. They walked on down towards the finish, past a jump made out of galvanized feed-troughs, through a hedge flattened out slightly for their convenience but rather unpleasantly downhill for Ruth's liking, and down to the recurring water, here slightly less impetuous, wider and shallower, with a gravelly bottom, and a rail set in front of it.

'At least they can smell home by now,' Thea said. 'Up the hill to all their friends and home and dry.'

'Hardly dry,' Jonathan said. 'Railway will immerse me here. I shan't be able to stop.'

'It's not a day for fast rounds, Jonathan,' his mother said severely. 'If you let Railway get out of hand you'll be asking for trouble. Super-caution is required.'

'At least if you fall off you'll only go splash,' he replied. 'Not crack or crunch.'

'You'll have to be dug out,' Peter said.

They ducked their heads into the driving rain and plodded back to the finish past the last point-to-point style brush fence and the finish markers. The first competitor had already started in the dressage arena, and several cars were parked round the show-jumping ring. Two tractors were busy helping pull horse-boxes through the gate at the bottom of the hill. The loud-speaker, flailed by the gusts of rain, loud and soft alternately, was calling for the early competitors, sounding hard-pressed and slightly annoyed.

'Such a lot of water—' Thea was saying.

'The rain's done it,' Mrs. Meredith said. 'These ditches are usually dry at this time of year, except the one that runs out of the wood, and that's generally just a trickle. Well now—' She glanced at her watch. 'You'd better get changed. You've got just under an hour. Jonathan goes first, then Thea, and you, Peter—Ruth last.'

Ruth felt damp and cold and frightened. It was no good pretending any more that it wasn't going to happen, because it assuredly was. She knew at the back of her mind she had been hoping for the event to be cancelled because of the weather, but the stewards were doggedly putting peat down over the take-offs, and the jump-judges were preparing for their long, tedious day with flasks of coffee and brandy and plastic boxes of chicken salad in the glove-lockers of their cars . . . in fact, the whole thing was under way. She followed the others back to the horse-box. She knew Toad could do it. She told herself that she had every reason for confidence. But the others knew Toad could do it too; it was herself. Herself. She shivered.

The rain eased off again and stopped. The sky cleared and the sun showed bleakly for a few minutes, shimmering over the sodden acres and rain-heavy trees. The earth smelled almost rank. It's all right, Ruth told herself. Toad was grazing on his halter, his white mane fallen forward. When she went up to him he lifted his head and nuzzled at her amiably, leaving green slobber down her jeans. 'You've got to do it for me,' she said to him. 'Pretend I'm Peter. You must.'

They got the ponies ready and changed and rode up to the dressage arena. It seemed to Ruth that the hillside was swarming with fantastically elegant ponies trying out their paces, every one a winner. The riders all looked confident and business-like. She put on a confident expression. Toad, by comparison with many of them, was half a cart-horse, and quite small. No excuse, she thought. Thea, riding beside her, looked both beautiful and competent, every hair in place, the pony quiet and shining. Thea didn't seem to get nervous. 'Nor am I,' Ruth told herself sternly. She knew the dressage test backwards, having marked it out on her bedroom floor and gone through it every night for the fortnight before camp until her father complained about the ceilings, the downstairs light fitting having fused at her 'Canter right between A and K' on the tenth evening. Looking towards the arena, she was pleased to see the current competitor's pony give a large buck half-way through its serpentine. The next one left the ring altogether at one point, which made her feel a lot better. Toad didn't seem to be at all excited, and was walking round without any fuss. Ruth was encouraged.

When it got near her turn, she went away and took Toad through a few preliminary manoeuvres. By experience she knew that too much beforehand made him too excited in the ring; he only needed a few circles at the trot, and no cantering. She missed seeing Jonathan and Thea, but got back just as Peter got the signal to start. She watched him trot up to the centre of the arena, make a flawless halt and take his hat off for a positively noble salute. Thank goodness girls didn't have to take their hats off, Ruth thought, having had so much trouble getting all her hair under control; an obsequious bow was all that was required. A couple of months back Peter wouldn't have dared take both hands off the reins when riding Sirius; Ruth was struck again by the pony's improvement. He certainly couldn't be described as relaxed, but he was perfectly obedient. As usual, Peter appeared to be doing nothing, but when he came close Ruth could see the fierce concentration in his expression. She could see that Sirius was bursting with vigour, and Peter was keeping him collected and smooth by what she assumed was pure will-power, for she could see no evidence of his holding him back. His hands were very light and still and Sirius was beautifully on the bit, but not pulling. The general impression was thoroughly professional. 'But that's what he is,' Ruth thought, remembering the dedicated schooling sessions day after day. 'A professional.' The boy was extraordinary. By comparison everyone else was just 'having a bash'. Quite a lot of his unpleasant father must have rubbed off on him, Ruth decided sadly, for his father was also a very thorough man, a glutton for work. It also occurred to her that her own performance, the next the judge would see, was bound to be rough by comparison, however well she did.

Mrs. Meredith appeared at her side, looking very happy, and

said, 'All set, Ruth? Keep up the good work—the others have done very well indeed. We're away to a flying start. I should think Peter is all set for a really good mark. I haven't seen anyone go better.'

'Well, I'm not very—'

'Ruth, you're perfectly capable of performing these exercises. They are really very basic. Stop pretending you're incapable. You're your own worst enemy.'

Ruth was jolted, and felt herself colouring up. Or was it a compliment? She looked up and saw Peter performing his last canter, incredibly slowly, his circle described with compass precision. His transition to 'working trot rising' was effected at the exact centimetre, his finishing halt and salute smooth, precise and dignified. Mrs. Meredith fairly glowed. Peter made his exit at the required free walk—perhaps a shade too free—and pulled up beside Ruth. He grinned at her and looked his normal stupid self.

'Good, wasn't he?'

'Perfect.'

'I've not seen anyone do better, Peter,' Mrs. Meredith said. 'The improvement is quite remarkable. I think we're going to get really good dressage marks between us.'

Waiting for her bell, Ruth could feel herself getting strung up. The fact that all the others had done well made it worse. She was going last every time, and would have this dire responsibility to uphold the standard. Peter was saying something, but she was no longer listening. Someone else loomed up in her vision and said, 'Are you going next? I've timed it well.'

It was Ted, wound up in his wet-weather motor-bike gear, looking like some one from outer space.

'Oh, Ted!' Seeing him, her noble resolutions, which had been in the act of deserting her, flooded back.

'I thought I'd roll along and see how you get on,' he was saying. 'Ducks'd do better, mind you. Mr. McNair rang and said to tell you he'd be over as soon as he could get away.' This was directed at Peter, and the last word coincided with Ruth's bell. She had an impression of Peter's face as she nudged Toad into his 'working trot sitting or rising', changing in a stroke from complacent triumph to doomed incredulity; Mrs. Meredith's the same, while Ted went on cheerfully about life-jackets being more use than crash-helmets. She was already in the centre of the arena and

148

pulling up, as if it were her bedroom at home, before she properly realized she had started. Reverent bow. She lifted her eyes and met the judge's, frowning through the steamy windscreen of his Land-rover at the bottom of the arena. Toad snatched at his bit, and she came to with a jolt, and proceeded to C, according to the pink instruction sheet, trying to shut out the expression on Peter's face, and give her whole mind to what she was doing. Now she was, in fact, actually doing it, it didn't seem nearly as difficult as she had imagined, and Toad was going quite amicably, lifting his knees up rather high but not pulling too badly. Even if she couldn't make him look like a desirable show-hack, she could at least get him to change pace in the right places if she tried hard enough. She con-centrated hard, and managed to be fairly accurate, but he was going much too freely and took about half the time to complete the convolutions that Peter had taken. Ruth, feeling that this was a better plan of campaign than trying to curb his ardour and getting the inevitable yo-yo reaction, completed the test with a feeling of relief. It wasn't good, but it could have been a whole lot worse.

She rode out, quite pleased, and discovered that Mrs. Meredith was obviously more worried about Ted's news than her perfor-mance, for she said, 'A very good effort, Ruth,' with a wan smile. Ruth thought another nip of whisky would do her good. Peter was sitting hunched in his saddle, his knees up on Sirius's withers, scowling horribly.

'Apparently I've said all the wrong things,' Ted said to Ruth.

'Yes, well, you've heard the story?'

'Yes. Peter said. But if he keeps up the good work, surely everyone will be happy, all will be forgiven? Of course. Some-thing else too,' he added. 'Or shouldn't I say?' He looked doubt-fully at Ruth, and decided to say. 'Your ex-nag is for sale. In the paper today.'

'Fly-by-Night?'

'Who else?'

'Oh, golly! Honestly? You're sure it's him?'

'Yes. The name and address is the same. I thought you'd like to know.'

'Oh, yes, of course. Oh heavens, I wish I could buy him—I wish—'

'Sanity, Ruth. I just thought you ought to know—I wasn't suggesting you bought him. But if that place is as bad as you say, he's bound to make a change for the better. It was supposed to be good news.'

'Well—' Ruth wasn't sure if it was or not. She looked at Peter, and decided that Ted had complicated a day that was already highly charged with responsibilities. The Fly-by-Night bit could, by Ted's argument, be considered good news, but the message for Peter was definitely off-putting. He looked white and suicidal again. Mrs. Meredith crossed over to him and said briskly, 'Stop being ridiculous, Peter. You'll have nothing to worry about if you carry on the same way as you've started. I doubt if anyone will beat your dressage. Now pull yourself together. You know perfectly well that I will cope with your father if necessary.'

She had recovered from Ted's blow, and was using her formidable energy to goad Peter. Ruth was full of admiration. All her ardour had returned; she was fairly bristling with the will to win.

'Now sit up straight, and think about what you're doing. We're depending on you. You can forget all the rest.'

Peter did as he was told.

'And you, Ruth! Both of you, if you put your minds completely to the job, can get very high marks today. I shan't be content with anything else. We can take care of all the other things afterwards, all together. Now go along to the jumping ring and see how long you've got to wait. Keep the ponies walking, and keep your mind on what you're doing. The Bandridge team is the one to watch—they've won for the last two years. And the East Mowbray is very hot. Off you go.'

Ruth, having thought she would be happy merely to get round, now discovered that she had actually got to win.

'If I don't do well, Sirius will get shot, and if I do, he'll be sold,' Peter said bitterly.

'But you must have thought of all that before?' Ruth said.

'Not really,' Peter said. 'I just thought of showing them, that's all. Not of the consequences.'

'Oh, shut up,' Ruth said, inspired by Mrs. Meredith. 'Just show them, and forget the rest.'

Peter shut up. They rode over to the jumping arena, which was thickly surrounded by spectators, in spite of the weather, joined up with Jonathan and Thea and told them the news. They rode round together, side by side, like a quadrille team, and Jonathan said to Peter, 'When we see him arrive, we'll keep him out of your way. Bamboozle him. Mother'll take him down to the booze tent, I bet. By the time he sets eyes on you you'll have scooped up all the rosettes.'

'Ride him down. Tread him in,' Peter said.

'That's not nice,' Thea said.

'He probably won't come anyway,' Ruth said. 'Forget him. Too busy making money.'

'I'll feel better when I get the jumping over,' Peter said.

'Let's go and watch the East Mowbray,' Jonathan said. 'They've got Guy Palmer in their team, and that girl with Mighty Midget. If they knock it all down, we've got quite a good chance of getting somewhere.'

The jumps were solid and honest and arranged in a figure-of-eight, without any tight corners or turns. But with the ground very slippery, there were not yet any clear rounds, and the turf was already ominously scored with skid-marks. They watched two competitors go round, demolishing quite a lot of the jumps between them, mainly by skidding into them, and Mrs. Meredith came up and said, 'Guy Palmer's only got twenty-five dressage penalties. Has he jumped yet?'

'No, he's next in. What about our scores?'

'They're not out yet. I think Peter might have equalled that though. I'll keep an eye on the board. Is this Guy? Yes. That's a fantastic pony.'

'It cost two thousand,' Peter said, who knew things like that.

It slipped into the first jump and knocked it down. Guy had a face like a poker, and turned away in a catlike circle to start again. His pony was a grey, not looking at all as if it was worth two thousand pounds, until it jumped the rest of the course clear. It was a very neat jumper, and Guy looked as if he didn't have anything to do. But Peter said, 'It's a pig to ride. We had it once.'

'He could well be the individual winner,' Mrs. Meredith said. 'He'll be the one to beat.'

Ruth glanced at Peter and saw him scowl again, and his lower jaw stiffen in a characteristic way. She stopped worrying about him and decided to worry about herself instead. Being in a team was a dreadful responsibility, especially now that the talk was all of winning. Ruth had never actually thought about winning, only not making a fool of herself. Now the others were getting ambitious, she could not help being aware of the fact that for their sake she mustn't make mistakes. The conditions being what they were, any one of them was likely to make a bad mistake, not only her. She couldn't tag along just making up the number; it was only the best three out of the four scores that counted, but she couldn't complacently accept that the one not counted was going to be her. If Guy Palmer could refuse at the first jump, who could depend on Jonathan or Thea going clear? It could all be a matter of luck in the end, the pony hitting a bad patch when it was taking off, or the rider getting blinded by a lump of mud. It would be terrible to let the others down by stupidity; act of God would be bearable, but only just.

The East Mowbray girl on Mighty Midget got the first clear round of the day.

'Her dressage wasn't up to much though', Mr. Milburn reported.

The other two members of the team made five faults each. This was the best team result so far. 'That's what you've got to beat,' Mrs. Meredith declared. 'And both Mighty Midget and Guy Palmer are top-class across country.'

'Like us,' Jonathan said.

Ruth felt sick. Ted came up and offered her a hot dog, which she declined; then she remembered to introduce him properly to Mrs. Meredith, who immediately enlisted his help in keeping an eye open for Mr. McNair. 'You know him? It would be such a help, because I'm keeping an eye on the scores and I want to watch them all jump—and we don't want him to see—er—Peter—before we can nobble him first. We must keep them apart, whatever happens, at least before the jumping. If he's coming, I think we'll be lucky if he doesn't turn up before we start the cross-country, because that's not until about three o'clock for us. Not much hope, I'm afraid. But if Peter jumps well, we'll be in a strong position by then.'

Ted was pleased to have a role in the day's operation and promised to keep his hawk-like eye on patrol. Peter's face went a shade grimmer, and they watched the team before their own demolish most of the course between them for a grand total of sixty-five faults. Jonathan rode up to the entrance and gave his number, looking suddenly very serious. Railway started pulling before he went into the ring, and Ruth could see that he wasn't a good horse for such conditions, not having the smaller pony's agility and powers of quick recovery. But Jonathan was taking no chances, and was taking him very slowly, holding him in hard. He looked to Ruth very competent and—suddenly—rather like his mother when she was on the war-path. She could see Railway's strength, and Jonathan's hands with the knuckles standing out white, the cob's muscle rippling down over his shoulders. . . . 'God,' she thought, 'I wouldn't like to ride that horse!' And Jonathan dropped his hands and Railway glided over the first jump and cantered on, striding out. Jonathan took him up again,

very tactful, and steadied him for a set of rails, upright and uninviting, and sent him on in the last three strides.

'Clear,' Thea said, waiting beside Ruth.

Ruth found she was holding her breath, and let it out. It did seem to matter dreadfully now. She didn't dare think about it. Think about how it mattered for Peter, and for herself by comparison it was nothing. Even Thea looked nervous now.

'It's like jumping on ice,' she said.

Railway was getting worried; he slipped going round the top of the field and pecked, and came up to the next jump, a wall, unbalanced. Jonathan seemed to gather him together bodily. Railway put a quick step in, took off too close and knocked the top brick off with a foreleg.

'One of our three lives,' Thea said.

'Oh, Jesus,' said Ruth. The more they took, the less left for her.

Railway came back down their side, now looking rather frightened, not liking it at all. It seemed to Ruth that it depended entirely on Jonathan to see him round; the horse, although very strong, was trustingly obedient, and Jonathan put him exactly right, strung up to superlative riding by the pressure of competition. Ruth had always considered him a rather slapdash rider compared to Peter, but now he was fully aware that it wasn't a slapdash sort of course. He came through the finish without any more faults.

'Good!' his mother said abruptly. Her eyes were now on Thea. She and her pony looked very dainty after Jonathan and Railway, and Bright Morning didn't seem at all ruffled or put out by the ground. Thea, as always, when she competed, was expressionless in what Ruth thought of as a very professional manner. No shouts of encouragement, mutterings of rage or blasphemy ever passed her cool lips. Once more it struck Ruth that she was a member of a very good team. Bright Morning went clear as far as the last jump, a triple-bar, where he slipped on take-off and took away the last pole. The better the others did the more awful Ruth felt her responsibility looming. She knew that she would truly have felt much better if Thea had made a hash of it, even while she was smiling and congratulating her.

'Oh, Peter!' He had everything to lose.

'Thank God we've got this far without that ghastly father of his arriving,' Mrs. Meredith said tightly. They all stood in a close row, feeling as one, even Ted. Ruth saw Guy Palmer pull up behind them and say to someone, 'We've got to watch these beggars. McNair's top in dressage so far, beat me by ten marks.'

Sirius entered the ring snorting and putting his feet down as if he would cleave the ground. He was pulling dangerously, but had no qualms like Railway, and was set on doing it his way, fast and wild. Clods of mud spattered the spectators as he went down to the first jump and cleared it contemptuously. Dangerously fast to the high rails, and Peter was just sitting there, watching, not interfering, only an imperceptible gathering together, a slight taking of the hands, and Sirius jumped about six feet in the air and landed half-way down the field, nearly to the next jump. The spectactors gasped and clapped spontaneously. Mrs. Meredith had her hands up to her face; her mouth was open. Ruth had run out of breath again, holding it, and had to make a conscious effort to breathe. Peter cleared the next three jumps, each with feet to spare, went round the top of the field and slipped in exactly the same place as Railway, leaving double score marks in the clotted grass. Like Railway Sirius recovered himself, came on to the wall wrong, stopped dead, and then jumped from a standstill. To the spectators he appeared to climb over the wall, but no brick fell. Peter, by an extraordinary feat of anticipation, stayed with him, not even losing a stirrup. Ruth heard Guy Palmer say, 'Bloody hell!' in tones of disgusted admiration, and Sirius came past them at his tearing pace, scattering liquid mud. Mrs. Meredith let out a groan, her face all screwed up in agony, but Peter, undismayed, let Sirius go on, and he cleared the in-and-out and the oxer beyond with his contemptuous, effortless skill, making it look as if all the others had been making difficulties where none existed. But for the last big triple-bar even Peter decided that he was going too fast for safety. He sat down hard and held Sirius in, collecting him together, but with such an intuitive knowledge of how far it paid to interfere that Sirius obviously thought he was doing it of his own accord, for he went on—'uncoiling', as Ruth thought of it—with a terrific gay enthusiasm, perfectly balanced and right for taking off, clearing the bars with what must have been a jump of six foot. The spectators burst into an unprecedented round of amazed applause at the performance and Peter rode out of the ring, pulling up, holding the back of his hand up to his mouth. Ruth saw blood, half pulled up—'Bit my tongue,' Peter said, but he was laughing. Ruth looked at him and he turned round to go to the ring entrance with her, suddenly not thinking of himself any more. 'It's all right,' he said urgently. 'You *know* he can—for you just as well as anybody. Don't *worry*!'

Ruth, eternally grateful, felt she was receiving the chaplain's last words on the way to the gallows. She went through into the ring, heard the steward bawl at her, turned back, checked with him, rode on. Toad was cantering already, before she had asked, boring down on his bit, not looking where he was going. She sat back and heaved him together, feeling a complete clown after

Peter's impeccable performance. Toad, surprised, came back to her, gave a small buck, and seemed to realize what they were about, for she felt him bunch up eagerly and saw his little red ears go forward, between which, like the target in a rifle-site, the first jump was squarely in view, looking perfectly harmless. She let Toad go on and he jumped it without hesitation. He was like a rocking-horse, held in, jumping forward in big bounds and snorting out with eagerness. He wasn't going to need any driving, only steering and steadying. If only she had a firmer seat, could do it like the others!—instead of being caught unawares, like a sack of potatoes. The big rails were there already and she hadn't placed him at all. He picked his own spot and she in her frantic eagerness to get it over kicked him on unashamedly, and thought she even shouted at him—whatever it was, it worked, for they were cantering fast on the other side, and she hardly aware of Toad's jumping at all. If it had fallen, she hadn't heard anything, and daren't look back. The rails were there too—how fast they must be going!—she flung her hands forward and they flew over it, landing with an almighty squelch. She felt the mud fly up her face, blinked, and looked for the next jump. Toad didn't seem to mind the mud at all, although she could feel his feet sliding about as he skated on.

She had been frightened of the wall, but Toad went round the top of the field without finding the slippery bit, met it exactly right and cleared it without trouble. Ruth felt far more optimistic and competent, as if getting so far without fault was all her own doing —perhaps it *was* all in the mind and she was as good as the others were always trying to tell her she was—but then the oxer seemed to arrive long before she was expecting it—yes, Toad was going far too fast! She took a hasty pull, felt Toad slither, recover, slither again, and take off much too late, bearing in mind the involuntary progress between strides. He hit the first part of the in-and-out and knocked it flying, landed in the middle and stopped at the second part, wisely, for he was in no position to jump. Ruth gathered herself together and rode him out of the side, while the stewards leapt forward to put the jump together again. She felt shocked, stopped literally in full gallop, disgraced, her confidence shattered. She walked Toad back slowly, waiting for her bell to go, not daring to look towards the ropes where the others were watching. Toad didn't seem to be bothered. The bell pinged, and she turned him and put him into a canter towards the jump again. This time he wasn't so impetuous; in fact she could positively feel his doubt; she pressed him on hard and he cantered on until the last stride and stopped. Not entirely surprised, she didn't come off, but she felt shattered.

Before the incident, she felt he had taken charge of her, and got her round without trouble, but now it seemed as if he had given up, and it was for her to take charge of him, and show him what to do. Perhaps with proper people it was like that all the way round, but with her it was a strange feeling, quite panic-making, as if she was all on her own.

'It's all right, Toad,' she said, just as Peter had said to her. 'You can do it easily.'

And to her amazement, knowing what was at stake, the panic gave way to a marvellous, motherly determination to see Toad through. She seemed to know what to do, sitting down firmly and driving him on. She just knew he wouldn't stop again, because of her own confidence, and he didn't. He jumped cleanly, hesitated in the middle, boggled slightly, and then jumped out in answer to her cries of encouragement and driving legs. The oxer appeared just when she expected it, not a moment too soon, and Toad swept over it obediently, and on with a huge bound over the triple-bar. Ruth felt marvellously accomplished, riding out to a scattering of applause, deeply grateful to have got round. When she had rejoined the others and seen their expressions it then came to her that she had done by far the worst round, with ten faults, putting them well behind the East Mowbray in spite of Peter's tremendous round. It hadn't really been very wonderful at all.

Mrs. Meredith however looked genuinely pleased and said, 'That was a very good effort, Ruth.' Ruth knew in a flash that Peter would have got Toad round clear, but it didn't hurt any more. By her own standards she had succeeded. Mrs. Meredith, for all she was a pot-hunter, was magnanimous enough not only to praise her, but to mean it.

'You have improved enormously, my dear. You really pulled yourself together after that fault, exactly the right attitude.'

'But we've gone down now, to the East Mowbray.'

'Just a temporary set-back. Remember the cross-country is still to come.'

Remember indeed! Ruth, incredibly, had quite forgotten. She looked across the soggy hillside, saw the ambulance lurking in the valley, saw the streamers of rain approaching out of a leaden sky, as if to eat up their little ant-like activity round the marked-out arenas, and felt her heart settle like lead. She realized she was frightened. If it was like that for the show-jumping, what was it going to be like galloping, and those fearful streams and ditches ever-filling, and the trees hanging weighted with rain, the great muddy ruts pulling and sucking? And Guy Palmer on their tail, not to mention Mighty Midget with his ferret-faced rider grinning broadly at her own ten faults? And Mr. McNair still to come as well . . . She rode back to the horse-box with Peter, who was still dribbling blood and trying to mop it off his black jacket.

'Only just come back from the cleaner's after last time,' he mumbled. 'Getting to be a habit. My gnashers have all come loose in their sockets.'

'Did you know you only got fifteen penalties for the dressage?'

'Yes. Good, aren't I?'

'What did I get? Do you know? And the others?'

'You got forty-five. Jonathan got twenty-five, Thea somewhere in between. Not bad at all. Mighty Midget got sixty, luckily, so we've got a bit in hand at the moment. But anything could happen across country. Nobody else is in striking distance—Bandridge made lots of lovely faults all over the place—'

Ruth, digesting the general triumph, noticed that she was definitely the weak member. In the total score, only the best three out of the four were counted, and she had to accept that the score to be discarded was very likely to be hers. In one way it was a bit of a relief to feel that her inadequacy didn't matter; in another it was a bitter disappointment. It was no good pretending that she hadn't had her dreams of beating all the others, in spite of everything, because she had. But now she saw, quite sensibly, that pure experience was invaluable. Just what she lacked. And just what was going to be needed in the afternoon, more than anything.

Peter, justifiably, was looking a lot happier. Mrs. Meredith was doing complicated calculations on her programme.

'We're level-pegging with Mowbray on show-jumping, and well ahead of them in dressage, mainly due to Mighty Midget's bad score. But if Mighty Midget is discounted as worst of the four— hmm—anything could happen. Depends on no disasters this afternoon. At least by the time you go, you'll know which obstacles are causing the trouble, and you'll also know what you have to beat, going after Mowbray—unless, of course, there are some un-expected results still to come. We can't count on anything.'

Ted, watching the entrance gateway, reported no sign of Mr. McNair.

'Not that he could be anything but impressed,' Mrs. Meredith said severely. 'Sirius is the leading individual so far. I shall tell him very strongly—' She had quite forgotten her original comments on setting eyes on the pony coming out of the horse-box. 'Come on, now, let's get a bite of lunch, see what Sally has put up for us. Water the ponies and tie them up with their hay-nets. Peter, hadn't you better go to the First Aid, and see about—'

'No. They're so keen,' Peter said. 'It's okay. Really.'

'I wouldn't be surprised if they have quite a lot to do later. The going couldn't be worse.'

'A cheerful lady,' Ted said to Ruth.

They changed into their cross-country jerseys and old anoraks and laid out Sally's spread in the back of the horse-box. Mrs. Meredith and Mr. Milburn returned to the comfort of the cab and the whisky flask and said they'd keep watch for Mr. McNair. Peter looked at his watch and said, 'With luck, he's not coming.'

'But it doesn't matter now,' Thea said. 'Now that you've done so well. You've already proved your point.'

Peter didn't look so sure. 'There's a little matter of having done what I wasn't supposed to do . . . he's a bit old-fashioned in some ways.'

'Bread and water for ten days,' Jonathan said. 'Confined to barracks. Fifty lashes.'

Ruth, not very logically, thought of Fly-by-Night being for sale. If they could get Mr. McNair in a good mood, she might have the nerve to ask him. . . . She felt edgy and nervous again, and not very hungry. She passed her food over to Ted. Gusts of rain rattled on the horse-box roof, and Mrs. Meredith brought her whisky flask round and gave them all generous dollops in their coffee. Ruth suspected it was a second flask, but it was beautifully comforting and gave her courage. The lunch break was short, and the first competitors were already gathering in the collecting ring for the cross-country, and the judges were driving out to their posts. The rain was coming and going in fits and starts. They all went out to assess the form, having plenty of time, plodging across the hill in their hard weather gear, hoods pulled up, to see what damage the nasty bit of water promised. Of the first three competitors, none reached as far as the formidable ditch, and the first one to arrive there fell in, plunged about and came out on the take-off side again. After that no exhortations of its game rider would persuade it to face the obstacle again, and it was retired when the next competitor came skidding into view out of the trees.

'That's Amanda Pickett,' Peter said. 'She'll do it.'

She did, in copybook style, and went skating out over the grass, clods and turf flying in all directions. The next comer skidded and hit the crossed telegraph poles in the lower field and then was eliminated at the sleepers into the wood, and the following rider disappeared in the wood and never came out again. The ambulance set off for higher pastures, wheels spinning, but could get no further than the top hedge, and a Landrover was sent to deputize. None of this was very cheering to the spectators.

'There's going to be a shortage of clear rounds,' Peter said unnecessarily.

'But a surfeit of drownings, maimings, heart-failure and sundry disasters,' Ted added.

Whilst they were watching, only half the competitors completed the course at all, and of these there were no clear rounds, and only one of five faults.

'Quite cheering really,' Peter said, as they set off back for the horse-box. None of the others said anything. Ruth was not at all encouraged. Peter walked with her and said quietly, 'Toad is good at this, you know. The conditions won't worry him like they'll worry Railway, for instance. Railway doesn't like it heavy. You saw him in the show-jumping. You haven't got nearly as much to worry about as Jonathan.'

'Haven't I?'

'Or me either. Sirius is such a show-off. Toad's got the most sense.'

'You've got something to worry about,' Ted said suddenly to Peter, touching his arm and pointing. 'That Mercedes—'

'Oh, God, yes. Go and tell Mrs. M., for Christ's sake. Head him off. And you too—will you? Beat him over the head with a bottle, if necessary. Anything. Please.'

'Get Milburn to bore him rigid. He's good at that,' Jonathan said.

'Just till I'm started. After that it doesn't matter.'

Ted departed at the double. The others went back to the horse-box. Peter tacked up very quickly, put on his number, crash-helmet and anorak and rode away down the field without saying anything else. The others, getting ready and tacking up, watched Mr. McNair skilfully intercepted by the receiving party and borne into the busy refreshment tent. There were six teams to go before them, but such was the number of eliminations that they went very quickly. And 'went' was the operative word. Ruth began to feel very frightened. She got on Toad and rode off between Jonathan and Thea.

'We must watch the bloody East Mowbrays,' Jonathan said. 'As far as I can see the order won't have changed. Is Mother totting it all up, or is she hung up with that interfering McNair bloke? What lousy timing! I thought Peter was going to get away with it.'

But Mrs. Meredith had escaped and was hurrying towards them. They went to meet her.

'Where's Peter?'

'He's keeping out of the way.'

'Good, we haven't told him. Jack's holding the fort—he's splendid there—I must try and see what you've got to beat—give you some idea how much you have in hand. Such a help. You don't want to ride to break your necks. There's Guy waiting to go now. If they do well, they might beat us. What a pity Peter isn't going first! It's going to be very difficult—'

'Guy's off now,' Jonathan said.

The grey pony, Catnap, lean and ugly, was completely undismayed by his task; his progress was followed with respect and grudging admiration by his adversaries. Jonathan was looking worried. A couple of hundred yards away, behind the horse-boxes, Peter was watching him too, walking Sirius round in steady circles.

'That's a clear round, if I'm not mistaken,' Mrs. Meredith said, frowning.

Mighty Midget, in pursuit, went even faster, and did not make a single mistake that any of them could see. Mrs. Meredith's frown deepened. She squinted up into the rain, her frizzled hair pressed down in corkscrews under her headscarf, a large raindrop hanging from the end of her arched nose. Little red veins stood out in her cheeks. She came over to Jonathan and said, 'Don't let Railway play you up. He only pretends, you know that.'

161

'It doesn't feel like pretending,' Jonathan said.

Ruth could feel herself shivering, or trembling, she wasn't sure which. The rain came across the bare hillside in almost horizontal gusts, right through their jackets and jerseys. The loud-speaker voice flared and went, shredded by the wind.

'What did he say?'

'A clear round.'

'Who? Guy or—'

'It's both of them,' Thea said. 'Guy and that girl.'

'Where's Peter? I hope he's watching what's going on. He mustn't—'

'Yes. He is. Over there.'

Mrs. Meredith was pencilling on her programme. 'That girl— Mighty Midget—had such an enormous penalty score for her dressage I don't think a clear round will make any difference— unless the others make a hash of it.'

'But they're not,' Jonathan said, watching.

'Ah!' Thea said. 'Five faults.' The third member of the team refused at the sleepers into the wood. It then jumped it clear and refused again at the big ditch. After that it jumped it and carried on clear, as far as they could see.

'Ten—but ten's good, today.' Jonathan said.

'The other one hasn't hit anything yet.'

'Are you ready, Jonathan?' his mother asked. 'Girths?'

The rain came pelting, as Jonathan's number was called. He could hardly see where he was going, riding down through the start.

'Don't hang about! Away you go!' The starter dropped his flag, and in the Landrover nearby the stop-watch was set. Railway went away at a tremendous gallop. Ruth, squinting up into the rain saw a flurry of mud, and the blue of Jonathan's jersey disappear through the far hedge.

'He hates this,' Mrs. Meredith said, stamping her feet with cold and impatience, 'Railway hates it.'

So do I, Ruth thought. Nobody in their right senses could possibly like it. It was crazy. She walked Toad about, his tail to the wind as much as possible. She pulled her girths up a hole, but her fingers were too cold to feel the buckle properly. Mr. McNair had come out of the refreshment tent and was groping for a pair of binoculars hanging round his neck. Ted was standing squarely in front of him, and Mr. Milburn was hanging back. Peter was still behind the horse-boxes, and Ruth couldn't tell if he had seen them. She rode down to Mrs. Meredith and said, 'Mr. McNair's coming.'

Mrs. Meredith, watching Jonathan, thrust her jaw out and said nothing. Thea was about to start. Jonathan was just going into the wood. Ruth saw him steady Railway for the big sleeper jump, thought for one ghastly moment that he was going to refuse, then saw him safely over and out of sight. She was getting worried about Peter. He had taken his anorak off and dropped it on the ground, ready to start, but his father was now quite close, advancing steadily towards Mrs. Meredith, smiling affably. Peter had seen him, Ruth noticed, and turned away. But he was the next to start, and would have to go down past his father to go through the start. But Ruth thought that if Mr. McNair tried to stop him, Mrs. Meredith, Mr. Milburn and Ted between them would stop him by force.

Thea got the flag and went away.

'That your boy that went into the wood, Mrs. Meredith? That ugly roan? Unmistakable brute. Peter gone yet? No?'

Mrs. Meredith didn't even glance at him, her eyes fixed on the jump out of the wood where Jonathan should be appearing at any moment. Ruth watched too, squeezed up with nerves, turning her face into the rain. She could feel the water trickling off her bundled up hair and down her neck. Thea was away like a streak across the bottom field. Railway appeared out of the wood very fast, and went over the ditch like a steeplechaser. But too fast—Ruth wasn't sure exactly what happened, but presumed that the sticky bank gave way under him, for suddenly he was on the ground, all legs, and Jonathan was shooting through the air on his own. 'Oh, Jonathan, you fool!' Mrs. Meredith hissed, her face convulsed. She banged her programme down with all its jottings blurring in the rain and almost spat at her companions, 'Thirty faults! Thirty!'

'Hard to get a clear round in these sort of conditions, my dear,' said Mr. McNair.

Jonathan wasn't getting up very fast, although someone had sorted Railway out and he was being held by the jump judge.

'Get up, boy!' Mrs. Meredith snapped. 'We don't want time faults as well. Get up! He'll be holding Thea up if he doesn't hurry.'

Thea was going fast up the hill towards the telegraph poles and the starter was looking for Peter. Jonathan was getting back on again and Thea was over the poles and heading for the sleepers. The steward was bawling for Peter, who appeared suddenly at a canter and went down through the collecting ring without a glance to either side. He shouted his number to the steward and went through the start without a pause, the starter dropping his flag as he went. It was perfectly timed, and Mr. McNair had not been given the faintest chance of stopping him, or even of speaking to him. Ruth, looking to see the reaction, saw that he was standing there looking as if he had been poleaxed, his mouth hanging open.

'Am I going mad?' she heard him say.

'You have been for years, Arthur,' Mrs. Meredith said crisply. She turned on her heel and came striding towards Ruth.

'Are you ready? We're still in it with a chance if you do a good round, Ruth. It all depends on you, do you understand? You must do your *very best*!'

Her eyes positively spiked Ruth, so that she felt herself transfixed, gaping back.

'Peter's ahead of you, just about riding for his life, the way things are. So you do the same thing, my girl. No risks, but as well as you possibly can. We all know you can do it. We're depending on you!'

She spoke very emphatically. Ruth wasn't quite sure if the woman wasn't a maniac at that moment, her stringy wet face held up with a sort of piercing, hypnotic fervour, the rain running down the sides of her craggy nose. Ruth saw Jonathan again, somewhere, but too deep down to describe where or how. It was just a reminder of how much she liked him, and how much it all mattered now; how much *she* mattered. The awful moment had arrived. The steward was shouting for her.

'Good luck, dear,' Mrs. Meredith said firmly. She was really quite sane after all. Ruth thought she must have been dreaming. She was already cantering through the start, dollops of rain flying up off Toad's mane into her face. The grass down to the first jump was flattened and slimy with mud and Toad's hooves cut in, tearing it up behind him. Lurch and snort, and they were over and heading fast for the grim ditch and rail. Ruth told herself that the others had all come this way safely; they had jumped it without any trouble and so could she. She did. Perhaps it wasn't so awful after all. But Jonathan had gone flying up by the wood, and had been ages getting up, looking from a distance only half there, and she wasn't to know if he had finished either. Perhaps that was exactly what Mrs. Meredith's harangue had been about—of course! Jonathan's would now be the discarded score, and hers would be the one that mattered! She had to pull up on those lousy dressage marks and make up for her ten-fault bungling in the show-jumping ring. God Almighty! No wonder Mrs. Meredith had looked so maniacal. Poor Jonathan, she thought irrelevantly. Poor Peter! And hooray for Toad, galloping with his dogged little ears pricked up into the rain. She shook her head to get rid of the water and saw the nasty little in-and-out right in her path, which somehow she had forgotten about. She was going much too fast and would go straight out the far side . . . she sat back and heaved in a thoroughly primitive manner, and Toad pulled up very quickly, jumped and stopped dead on the other side, nearly shooting Ruth over the top. She turned him and showed him the way out, which fortunately faced back towards the collecting ring and wasn't very high; he boggled at it for a moment, then jumped out very respectfully, about two feet higher than necessary, which nearly shot her off for the second time.

'Idiot!' she shouted at him, and pressed him on, up into the rain again, making up time where the ground was uphill and fairly firm. Lucky he was so fit. They went through the gateway and in a big surprised arc to the nasty rail and drop down into the cart-way. She pressed him on, feeling his surprise at what he was being asked to do; the landing was knee-deep goo, and splashed up in great gouts all over her chest and face. She spared a quick hand to smear at her eyes, steered him through the gap in the hedge and was away up the hill to the crossed poles and the horrible sleepers at the top. He pounded on, pulling now, getting the hang of the thing, his excitement mounting after the long, cold wait. Soon, Ruth thought, she wouldn't have to urge him on, but try and hold him back. He reached out, nearly pulling her arms out of their sockets, and she let him go on. No sign of Peter ahead, who must be going great guns, no bodies by the wayside . . . they were all home and dry and she was going to make it too, the way she felt. It was marvellous! *Of course* she could do it! Whyever had she been such a wet, hopeless ninny—God Almighty! Toad lunged at the crossed poles and hit them a terrific crack with his back legs. They weren't knock-down, so it didn't matter, but it gave him a fright.

'Pick 'em up, you old fool!' she said to him. 'You can't afford to hit the next one.' It looked dark into the wood, and the sleepers were black, a solid wall. It was hard work getting up steam to clear them, uphill and uninviting. She felt his doubt, and urged him on. Wet leaves crashed her face and she smelled the heavy, sodden rankness of thick woods, slimy bark grazing her knees, green smears on her pale jods, thick padded leaves underfoot like treading on kippers, silent pudgy ground . . . she was dreading the big ditch, Jonathan's downfall. It didn't matter how you got through though, only to *get* through; it didn't have to be gracious, impressive, like a Badminton winner. . . . She could hear the water running. She pulled, steadied, and there it was, the far bank looking far worse than the water itself, all cut away and gleaming wet and miles out of reach. Toad shortened his stride and his head went up, amazed. Remembering Peter, she caught hold of his mane and dug her heels in and urged him on with her whole body. The black, glistening bank seemed to rear above her—Toad was in, plunging and threshing through, soaking her to the skin, the water right up to her knees. She got a mouthful, like drowning, gulped, and felt Toad slice at the bank, lunging up for the grey sky and the rain. God Almighty! The saddle was wet and slippery as soap and she was sliding off backwards. The long white mane tangled in her fingers was a rope for saving her, the only thing. What had Ted said about life-jackets? And then they were out in the open and galloping very fast over blurred grass. Ruth's eyes were full of water and she had lost a stirrup. She groped for it, and realized she was heading back to the start, down the hill, instead of along the edge of the wood. She pushed her right knee in hard, pulling Toad up carefully, swinging him round again back to the wood. He slackened pace, thinking he had been going home, and now to be faced with the wood again . . . but it was only the gate this time, hanging open. His hooves boomed alarmingly on the sleeper bridge, and they were back in the soft gloom again, the black peaty track, all mashed and trodden, unrolling ahead. Time to breathe. Ruth kept her head down, steadying the pony, collecting him as well as she could, ready for the sudden jumps, cunningly in wait. To be ready, not to be surprised—that was what mattered.

They did them beautifully, and Ruth knew that it was quite a lot due to her good riding, because she was ahead of herself, prepared, expecting, anticipating—not all panicking and hanging on for dear life which was how she remembered most of the similar competitions on Fly-by-Night. Toad, in spite of the conditions, felt extraordinarily safe and confident, in fact was probably too confident, pulling hard. She realized that her shoulders were beginning to ache, and there was the very nasty jump out of the wood looming up. . . . She tried to steady Toad a bit more, but he wouldn't have it, pulling eagerly. The trees were thinning. The wet peat splattered behind them, and she saw the red and white flags, the gap yawning into daylight at the top of another slimy bank, poached hoof-marks like pits, and the impossible rail balanced across the sky. There was nothing to bite on, to take off from. Toad, clawing over the mud with great springs from his hind-quarters, hurled himself over the top but sent the rail flying in the process. He was on his knees, sprawling. Ruth grabbed at his mane again and shouted at him. She had a glimpse of the stewards' faces, felt Toad scramble together again beneath her—great snorts of effort and heaving shoulders, then they were away and flying down the hill at a terrifying rate, much too fast.

It was hard to stop him now, flying for home and downhill, and Ruth didn't feel she had much strength left. She tried to pull the pony together, but he had a mind of his own—'a boy's pony', as she had heard him described so often—what would Peter be doing now, for Heaven's sake? She used all her strength to try and slow him for the feed troughs, but he snatched at her hands again and seemed to go even faster. He jumped them in his stride and bore down towards the hedge, a far more formidable obstacle, and Ruth felt frightened. Her hands were numb and the wet reins slithered through her fingers. She sat back, praying hard, and the big hedge reared up. Toad skidded wildly in the poached take-off and crashed through it with a great tearing of branches. The landing was a sea of mud and peat, like porridge, splattering up in all directions, and Toad checked slightly and Ruth pulled at him again, dreading the water at the bottom.

'You fool! You fool!' she stormed at him, and heaved, and he gave his head a shake, rather wearily, and she felt him come together again and take notice. She sat into him and used all her strength, and he dropped his nose and cantered on very obediently, still keen but not wild. It mattered terribly, for the rail in front of

the water was going to be very difficult, and at flat gallop he would just have gone through it. Ruth didn't want another fault. It was up to her this time, the riding part that mattered. There was scarcely any landing beyond the rail, only the swollen stream all muddied up and uninviting. Ruth felt Toad disliking it, but he was beautifully in hand now, just right, and she could drive him on in the last few strides, placing him slightly to one side where it was firmer.

'Go on!' she bawled at him desperately, and he jumped with

intense care, not liking it at all, picking up his back legs as if the rail would bite him. It stayed in place, and Toad was in the water, great heavings and boundings and snortings again as he struck out for home, up the other side in a great wet flurry like a golden Labrador.

'Thank God! Thank God!' Ruth felt herself praying; the nasty bit was past, and she could see the people knotted over the hill beyond and the finishing flags gleaming white through the driving rain. Water flew everywhere, Toad's hooves smacking the soggy turf, and the harmless last jump came up and Toad felt to Ruth as if he would eat it up, reaching into it, the matted black twigs scattering out of his way, and the home run ahead—now he could gallop on as fast as he liked. Ruth leaned forward and urged him on, and he tore up the slope, and she felt as if she would burst with pure and glorious gratitude for her lovely performance. The flags shot past, some rash spectators disappeared in a smattering of mud, and she was pulling up, not without some difficulty, looking for the others, and remembering all the other problems— Mr. McNair and Jonathan's fall and—but none of her own! She could not help grinning, laughing like a maniac.

The first person she saw was Thea, riding towards her. 'What did you do? Did you go clear?'

'No, but only one—knock-down!' Ruth had no breath, trying to pull up. 'Out of the wood.'

'Same as me. Is that all? I say, that's magnificent! That's only ten! Peter went clear! Can you believe it? He nearly caught me up at the end. Nobody will beat that! Come and tell Mrs. Meredith—'

'What—what does Mr. McNair think about it?'

'Well, he can only think one thing, surely, if he's the owner of the individual winner—'

Could he? Knowing him, Ruth wasn't quite sure. Mrs. Meredith was advancing eagerly, Ted grinning behind her.

'What did you do, Ruth? You were never clear? I didn't see you knock anything—'

'Yes, the rail out of the wood. But that's all.'

'My dear, that's wonderful! Really magnificent! Oh, how splendid! We really should come out on top with a score like that —knocking out Jonathan, you see, I make it—'She started totting up again on her programme, which was all soggy and disintegrating. 'It depends on—mm—I must go and wait by the score-board. There may be time faults, I'm not sure about that—oh, well done, both of you!'

In her excitement she seemed to have abandoned Peter to his fate. Ruth could see him talking to his father, still on Sirius, plastered in mud, very serious. Jonathan was nobly standing by, but when he saw the girls he came towards them, leading Railway.

'How's it going?' Ruth asked.

'Seems fairly amicable. I thought I'd leave them to it. After all, what can the old man say? Peter's individual winner by miles.

How was Toad?' He turned to Ruth and she beamed down at him.

'One knock-down!'

'God, I knew it! The only failure round here is the D.C.'s own little lad. She won't even speak to me.'

'Are you all right? You went a terrible cropper. What happened?'

'I don't know. My arm hurts. I couldn't have got on again if that old geezer hadn't bunked me up. That's why I lost so much time. And after that I couldn't steer properly. Disaster all the way.'

He smiled, looking rather sad at the same time, and then said, 'If you're going to cool your animals off, will you take Railway too?'

Ruth took his reins. She thought he looked shaken and a bit blueish. Perhaps Ted thought so too, for instead of coming to speak to Ruth as he obviously intended, he stayed with Jonathan. Ruth heard him say, 'Do you want your coat?' as she rode away,

and she realized that they were all soaked right through to the skin. The rain was still coming down in buckets. But funnily enough she felt warm and glowing, as if she had had another shot of Mrs. Meredith's whisky. Thea looked the same. They rode round together, cooling the ponies off, comparing notes, and shortly they were joined by Peter.

'Hail the winner!' Thea said. 'How does it feel to be proved right?'

'A nice change,' Peter said. 'He was so surprised he couldn't think of anything to say.' He turned to Ruth and said, 'How did our Toad go, then ? If your finishing burst was anything to go by—'

'One knock-down.'

Peter's eyebrows went up in genuine amazement and he gave her a hard, almost angry, look. Ruth grinned at him. Then he smiled too, a bit wryly, and said, 'That's a turn-up for the book!' Ruth knew exactly what he was thinking, but didn't say anything to rub it in. And almost immediately he said perfectly genuinely, 'Well done! I had a feeling there was a pounding of hooves right behind me. What's happened to Jonathan ?' He indicated the rider-less horse between them. 'Drowning his sorrows ?'

'He looks a bit wonky, hurt his arm.'

'Railway was all over the place,' Thea said. 'I nearly caught him up—I thought there was something wrong. When I got home his old ma was giving him hell and he said his arm had gone numb, and she said, 'Rub it, then,' in a really dragonish voice—far more interested in watching you, Peter, and taking no notice at all of your poor old dad, who was gibbering away like a maniac and saying all the things he was going to do to you—has he changed his mind ?'

'I'm not sure. It might all crop up later, but at the moment he's a bit squashed—doesn't quite know what to say. Someone came up and asked him if Sirius was for sale while we were still talking, and I said no, he wasn't, more than our reputation was worth—that's what Dad had said before, so he couldn't argue, but he was a bit mad, I could tell. Anyway, I'm not going to let him sell him, however much anybody offers. I'll shoot him first.'

'Who, Sirius or your dad ?'

Peter grinned.

Ruth said, 'You want to get Mrs. M. to give your dad a blast—not to sell him, I mean. She makes everybody do what she wants.' (Even to getting her round that course—by hypnosis. Ruth remembered the maniacal glitter in her eyes at the starting-post, blinking into the rain, exhorting her to ride to win.)

They compared notes on their various rounds and rode back to the horse-box. There was nobody else there. They untacked the ponies and put their rugs on and bandaged them up and loaded them back into the horse-box, Peter doing Railway as well. Then they changed into whatever dry clothes they could find and sat in the cab watching the last distant competitors going round the

172

course, and eating the last of Sally's sandwiches. Peter switched the ignition on and got the heating and the windscreen wiper going, and helped himself to another nip of Mrs. Meredith's whisky, and they sat congratulating themselves, warm and fuggy and, Ruth discovered, really rather sleepy. She felt fantastically happy. Peter handed her the whisky bottle and she took one mouthful. The taste was beastly but it felt so lovely afterwards.

'We must have won,' Peter said. 'We can't go home—pity—because we've got all those lovely cups and rosettes to collect.'

The last competitor had finished. The jump judges and stewards were coming back up the hill in their Landrovers and estate cars, wheels spinning and engines whining. The tractors were at work towing home-going horse-boxes out through the gateways. Mrs. Meredith appeared unexpectedly and suddenly out of the rain, flinging open the cab-door and blasting them with cold rain and invective.

'What on earth do you think you all look like, for Heaven's sake? You've got to go and get your *prizes*! You look a dreadful load of scruffs! Now get out and put your jackets on again—get that mud off your boots. Comb your hair! Ties! Good gracious, you've got to *look* like winners. Where's Jonathan got to?'

They scrambled out, shivering, trying to hide the whisky under Mrs. Meredith's driving gloves.

'Where *is* Jonathan?'

No one had seen him.

'He's crawled under a hedge to die somewhere,' Peter muttered, scrubbing the gouts of mud off the front of his tie with Sirius's tail-bandage. 'And I don't blame him.'

'I make it that you've beaten the East Mowbray by five points. The scores are up on the board—subject to confirmation. But I'm pretty sure we've made it. And Peter is individual winner, with Guy Palmer second. Ruth, your hair—do something about it. Where is Jonathan?'

Mr. McNair was talking to Mr. Milburn, actually smiling. Everyone was congregating round the Secretary's tent and the score-board, and Mrs. Meredith chivvied them out. The loud-speaker was confirming the results: 'First, Maybridge Hunt Branch, with one hundred and twenty-five penalty points. . . .'

Wet clapping and wind-blown cheering loomed on the wind and they went to get their rosettes and silver cup from a large aristocratic man muffled up in riding mac and a deer-stalker hat. Peter took Jonathan's, and they passed the East Mowbray on their way back, going up for their inferior seconds. Guy Palmer gave Peter a murderous glare and Peter smiled back. Presently he had to go up for his own cup, and rosette.

'Wherever has Jonathan got to?' Mrs. Meredith said crossly.

Mr. McNair was clapping briskly, smiling. 'Here's Ted. Perhaps he knows. Where've you been, Ted? Seen Jonathan? We've lost him.'

'Oh, no, he's not lost. They took him away.'

'Who did?'

'The blood-wagon. Broken collar-bone. I thought you knew.'

'Oh, really!' Mrs. Meredith said crossly. 'He might have had the sense to wait till we got home! Didn't he tell them? They could just have done it up for now and I could have taken him in tonight, at home.'

'He did say, but they insisted. They were going in with a concussion and a hammered thumb-nail, and I think they wanted all the seats filled. Made them happy. He didn't stand a chance.'

'Now I shall have to—oh dear, we can't keep these ponies here all wet and hungry—hospitals take ages. I'll have to drive the box home and come back—'

'No, not at all. I'll drive down and wait for him and bring him home. Don't you bother,' Mr. McNair said. 'A pleasure.'

'Oh, Arthur, thank you—that's very kind!'

They were suddenly all beaming and looking very pleased and happy. Ruth thought they were rather funny, but was pleased the way things had worked out. She had quite a lot to thank Mrs. Meredith for really. She felt terribly tired. She looked at Peter and Thea, and saw Peter yawn as well, behind his silver cup. He wouldn't have to do all his riding at night now, which would be a help. They went back to the horse-box and crammed in, feeling the ponies' warmth meet them, and the comforting rumble of the engine starting up, dispensing further fug. Ted had roared off on his motor bike, sending her a final wink; Ruth thought she had something else important to think about, but couldn't remember what it was. She thought of Jonathan, pale and brave, having his collar-bone set—poor Jonathan, and his mother saying, 'Rub it'. She was glad her mother wasn't like that. It had been a marvellous day. She couldn't remember one like it in all her life.

17

I T did seem a bit stupid, when the Meredith caravan had no less than six berths and was warm and dry and so utterly comfortable, to go back to the trailer and sleep amongst the puddles on damp lilos—or so Ruth and Thea thought.

They had called in for bedtime cocoa, and got snugged down, very tired and warm, lapped with plushy cushions, and now couldn't bring themselves to go.

'Don't,' Peter said. He was drinking cocoa out of his Junior Individual cup, sitting on the end of Jonathan's bed. Jonathan was in bed with his arm strapped up, looking very uncomfortable, but too well-brought-up to complain.

'I mean, don't go,' Peter said. 'Sleep here. We don't mind, do we, Jonathan? We're not fussy.'

'It's not in the rules,' Jonathan said.

'Too sexy, you mean?' Peter said.

'Yes, of course. Ma'd go potty, if she found them here. Sleeping, I mean. She's coming back—she said.'

'To tuck you up? Don't you believe it. She's not bothered about you. "Rub it," she said—to a man with a fracture. I ask you! She was more worried about Railway, with no one there to see to him. She won't bother—'

There was a crisp knock on the door and Mrs. Meredith put her head round.

'Can I come in? I've brought you some sleeping pills, Jonathan. Don't get up, Peter. Oh, hullo, you two. You're all very snug in here, I must say. Oughtn't you girls to be thinking about bed?'

'They are,' Peter said. 'They want to sleep with us.'

'In here, we said, idiot,' Thea said. 'Not the same thing at all.'

'Your trailer is a bit wet, I must say. I've had a look round all the quarters tonight. Four of the smaller children are sleeping in the mess tent—the rest seem all right. I think it *would* be a good idea if you slept in here. In fact, I was thinking of moving in as well, to keep an eye on Jonathan. He ought to be at home really, but there's no one there tonight. We can let down the double bed and you girls can use that, Peter can have the bunk over the top, and I'll move in over Jonathan. All right—go and get your things then. Hurry up. Peter can help me with the beds. Come on, boy. Don't sit there gawping.'

Ruth and Thea had to escape quickly, the sight of Peter's consternation too funny to contain. The prospect of the Meredith luxury was gorgeous, even with Mrs. Meredith as chaperone.

'She's not so bad really, in spite of everything we say about her,' Ruth said.

'She expects a lot of you,' Thea said, 'but it works. You find you can do it.'

'Yes.' That was it exactly. 'She doesn't treat you like—she treats you like an equal.'

'And even not fussing—it's better, sometimes, when they say "Rub it" for a fracture, rather than go on for ever about not getting your feet wet and sitting on damp grass and—'

'And letting Peter ride Sirius. It made everything come right.'

'Yes. She's not bad really.'

Lying in the double bed, warm and rainproof, Ruth found that she didn't sleep, in spite of being so tired. Everyone else seemed to be asleep; she could hear Jonathan's breathing, heavy and regular, see Peter's arm dangling down from above, the fingers relaxed, his watch still in place, the luminous hands pointing to half-past eleven. It had been a wonderful day, the best day of her life, right to the very end, grooming Toad in the dusking barn and giving him his well-earned feed, leaning her cheek on his satiny withers and smelling his lovely pony smell and remembering how he had gone for her, as well as for Peter. And Peter had been so angry— jealous—just for a minute, and then he had stopped himself and smiled. And, remembering Toad, Ruth recalled the other thing. It spiked her, all amongst the deep content. Fly-by-Night.

She saw Peter's arm lift up and turn— he was looking at his watch.

'Peter!' she whispered.

He leaned over, peering down at her. 'What's up?'

'I meant to ask your father, when he was in a good mood, and I forgot—that man has put Fly-by-Night up for sale again. You know, the beastly man. Would your father buy him, if I asked? Would you ask him?'

'Yes. If you want.'

'Was he in a good mood? When you left him? I mean, is it all right with Sirius?'

'Yes, I think so. Doing so well—he couldn't really get narked, could he? I got a lecture, but only for the sake of form—no steam in it.'

'And can you keep Sirius?'

'Yes. To try for Wembley next year. He said I could.'

'That's marvellous!'

'Ruth.' It was Mrs. Meredith. Ruth was silent, wishing she had kept quiet. She had assumed, from the total silence, that Mrs. Meredith had been asleep too.

'There's a child wanting a new pony—Fly-by-Night would be just the type for her, if he's for sale again. She's good, she could cope. Good home. Remind me in the morning. I'll sort it out for you.' Her voice was just as brisk as ever, but muted. Kindly, Ruth would have said. 'Now go to sleep. Go to sleep both of you. You've a lot to do in the morning.'

A lot to do! But I've done it, Ruth was thinking. I've done everything. She slept.